CANCELLATION
BY DEATH

CANCELLATION BY DEATH

A VICTORIA BOWERING MYSTERY

DORIAN YEAGER

ST. MARTIN'S PRESS
NEW YORK

Design by DAWN NILES

Library of Congress Cataloging-in-Publication Data

Yeager, Dorian.
    Cancellation by death / Dorian Yeager.
        p. cm.
    "A Thomas Dunne book."
    ISBN 0-312-08152-9
    I. Title.
PS3575.E363C36   1992
813'.54—dc20   92-26161
                                        CIP

10 9 8 7 6 5 4 3 2

This book is dedicated to Broadway star Fran Stevens, whose illumination and belief always made everything better than all right.

ACKNOWLEDGMENTS

Jeremy, who allows me to mother him—sometimes; Gerald and David, who married me even though they knew better; Robert and whoever else—if any—volunteered or considered it; Deb, Elyse, Jen, and Kristie, who suffered through it all, several times; Big Bill, enforcement guy; Tom and Deb Prather's Dutch Apple Theatre folk who cast me despite everything; Adnan, for keeping me humble; Mitchell & Associates for supporting the congenitally red-haired; Miss Elle's Homesick Bar and Grill, which always has a stool open for the word-blocked; Stuart Wood, who ought to get more work on "The Guiding Light" since he's so good at guiding me; Dee, Dennis, and McAleer's for comfort; Pat Yeager Ureneck for never snitching; Mom and Dad, who provided me with the basic genetic material to embarrass them; literary agent Fran Lebowitz, who actually returns my calls, as does my editor, Reagan Arthur; role models Nonnie, Betty, and Mom Fink; and every other person in the world I ever hugged or told "I love you" because I meant it. You know who you are and you'll doubtless be hearing it again. Ad nauseam.

Oh. And Sean Connery, Tom Selleck, and Maximilian Schell, because this is *my* book and I can thank whomever I want even if they never call, they never write . . .

CANCELLATION BY DEATH

PROLOGUE

All professions have their problems. The trouble with being an actor is all the time spent asking yourself, "Why not me?"

The rest of the time is dawdled away asking yourself, "*Why* me?"

In a stage play, performers like me just love getting murdered—the earlier, the better. In *Something's Afoot,* my/Lady Manley Prowe's smoking electrocution was the fabulous climax to act 1. Very flashy—strobe lights and much twitching and writhing. In the notable Shamokin, Pennsylvania, summer-stock production of *Deathtrap,* I/Myra spent leisurely dead time flat on the stage even before intermission. Aside from the Twilight Show, in which a suspicious non-union fly chose to waltz all over my face, it was great. I got paid the same as all the other actors, had to learn only half as many lines, and spared myself (and the long-suffering choreographer) a lot of frustration. I got my share of the applause at curtain call, and caught up on my correspondence during the second act.

Directors call me a "natural" actor. That means I am far too lazy to study my craft. Likely, the only reason I do so well getting performing work is a genetic kink—and I have a load of those. Some are just more easily ignored than others.

In explaining one of the more obtrusive family traits, it would be incorrect to say that I "see things clairvoyantly." It's probably more that I notice things, and by noticing I draw some very intriguing conclusions. My father, a scientist, says I'm a witch. My mother says I take after her side of the family, which is clogged with aunts and cousins who often have the unique opportunity to catch up on gossip with dead people. Being luckier than I, my relatives' dead people are just specters.

The corpses I run across don't walk, or send messages to loved ones. They just lie there. Believe me, it's nothing like a play. Which, in turn, leads to my moonlighting job as the Uri Geller of the bar-mitzvah business—a subject I will cover at great length later on.

Real-life murder is, alas, less gratifying cocktail-party chatter than the dramatic arts. Unlike in stage homicide, the blood doesn't always wash out, and finding the body never goes according to the script. And as for the victim, no matter how interestingly one dies, very few spectators applaud. At least, not publicly. On the other hand, the certifiably (and clinically) dead actors usually rake in more floral tributes than we of the eight-times-a-week variety. But then, we get to come back to die again and again.

I don't know. Being an actual victim is a real attention-getter, but—on the whole—this time, I was glad someone else got the part.

CHAPTER
ONE

You took the microwave."

I believe my deeper-than-usual voice conveyed the intended rationality, despite the urge to become physically, uncontrollably violent. I am, after all, a paid-up member of the American Federation of Television and Radio Artists. On the other hand, I was speaking to my soon-to-be-ex husband, who has a terrifying talent of making my every utterance sound vapid. Actors have an enormous tendency to be easily damaged. The lucky ones find a veneer to repel that sort of thing. My veneer still needs some work.

"You hate microwaves, Vic," Barry responded reasonably. He leaned forward, very sincerely, I thought, on the terribly tidy surface of his oversized classic desk—the one I'd unearthed in a crappy office-supply place just off Times Square and finagled for a song and just the barest minimum of tap dancing—and looked hurt. Gnawing guilt welled up within me, as it always did when presented with the vaguest intimation of his disappointment. It occurred to me that no one in the world knew this as well as dear Barry. This revelation wrestled down the guilt and thrust forward a mad desire to reformat the hard disk on his computer. Fortunately, I remembered that my résumé was on it. Instead, I lit a cigarette, and crossed my legs. They're inordinately long, and one of Barry's weaknesses.

"Let me rephrase that, Counselor." I blew a cloud of smoke. Barry hates that: the smoke and the amateur lawyer-talk. Childish? You bet, but I knew if I didn't play hardball I'd be on my hands and knees that evening futilely searching for such remaining items as my living room rug. "You took *my* microwave. While I was out of town for a lousy three days, *you* took the microwave that *my* parents gave *me* for *Christmas.*" A tendril of red hair escaped from the comb holding it off my face, and curled—as though it had a mind of its own (which I think it does)—unerringly into my eyeball. Irritated, I tucked it back. "You wouldn't let me have a tree, and then you took *my* one lousy Christmas present." Best intentions aside, I believe I glowered. "Does that sound particularly chivalrous to you, O officer of the court?" Actually, upon reflection, I'm quite certain I was glowering. I'm also a member of the Screen Actors Guild.

"Well, if it means that much to you, take it back. It's only an ap*pli*ance." Barry's big square hands laced professionally over the manila folder he'd been studying. A glint of pink scalp showed through his dark curly hair. You'll have to trust me: it's very sexy. "I thought we both wanted an amicable divorce. But you take it." There was that sincere look again. I was not going to be taken in; I'd seen him practicing it in the mirror too many times, shaving extra close before a court appearance. Still, if he saw any sign of weakness (and I had bucketloads of that), my microwave would be but another fond memory.

"It is not *an* appliance, it is *my* appliance. I am doing a god-awful production of *Steel Magnolias* somewhere in the armpit of the Poconos, and every time I get back to the apartment, something electrical is missing." I was feeling righteous indignation at that point. There was no going back. "The first week it was the computer and the TV; the second, the coffee machine and the toaster-oven; the third week the iron, coffee grinder, and the stereo. I thought you were finished when I discovered the waffle iron missing—the waffle iron, Barry, you don't know how to make a damned waffle, you strain yourself slicing a bagel—but now I don't have a thing left that plugs into the wall." I was so worked up, I'd forgotten to blow smoke around, so I puffed three or four times in quick succession. He got up and calmly cracked the window behind his chair. Mollified by his discomfort, I delivered my WASPiest coup de grace. "It would have been well-bred of you to have asked."

I knew it wasn't nice of me, but you have to understand: I've never won an argument with Barry the barrister over anything. He's a trained professional. His face drained of color and he got that little twitch at the left side of his mouth. I held my face in perfect composure, enormously gratified by the dead-on hit.

Life can be good, even during the shattering demise of an ill-conceived marriage. Even when you are the dumpee.

"All right," he said, "we will divide evenly." Barry settled back into his leather wing-back desk chair. "But I would like to remind you that you got to keep the rent-stabilized apartment, and I *would* have asked about taking things if you were ever in town."

"Point taken," I conceded—though, you ought to know, my apartment is a north-facing first floor, that, at high noon, is as dark as your average tin mine. The bedroom is so small I have to kneel in the center of the bed to make it. Nonetheless I persisted, "Though I don't know what you would have done with the apartment, since you've bought a co-op which, I'm certain, has somewhere within its sunny and spacious seven rooms my out-of-town telephone number." I smiled affectionately, radiating benevolence as I studied the books lining the walls. And, while I had his attention, I slid in, "I need the iron."

5

"So do I. You're not the only person in the city who has to be well-groomed, you know." Uh-oh, petulance was rearing its ugly head.

"I know that, darling." I steeled myself for yet another thing I'm bad at: negotiating. "Look, you keep the computer, I want the damned iron. Cost of the computer, approximately thirty-two hundred dollars; cost of iron, approximately thirty-two dollars. Net gain for you: three thousand one hundred sixty-eight bucks." He was considering. I pressed my mathematical advantage. "You send your shirts out to be laundered anyway."

"Fair." Barry leaned back slightly. "Now, I should have the stereo, since you sing."

"Excuse me?"

Attorneys should not be allowed to marry non-attorneys. Actresses should not be allowed to marry anyone at all. It's too dangerous for everyone involved. I can cry at will, but for some unknown reason consider it poor sportsmanship.

Barry made strong eye contact. Attorneys learn that (and the fact that there *is* no such thing as poor sportsmanship) their first year of law school. "You can sing to yourself, I can't. I'm human. I deserve music in my life." He was serious. I could see it on his face.

"Oh, for heaven's sake, all right." I collapsed back into the chair opposite him for the heavy negotiating. "But I get the coffee machine, coffee grinder, boom box—I *do* need to rehearse audition music from time to time—and *my* microwave." Naively, I was beginning to think I had a chance, after all.

"Sweetheart, you know I can't cook." Barry's shoulders slumped slightly and he let his large brown eyes sag into the helpless look I've always been a sucker for. "Without the microwave, I'll probably starve to death." Wham. Doomed. Wrongo. I was, again, beaten by a pro.

"All right." I was running out of resolve. "But I want a voucher for five lunches and five dinners. I pick the restaurants." If he didn't agree, I was going to cry purposefully.

Well, I think it would have been on purpose.

"Done."

Now you shouldn't get the wrong idea here. Barry and I love each other about as much as two people from different planets can. He has a career and a future, I'm in theater; he's a Jew from the Midwest, I'm an Episcopalian from New England; he's disciplined, I'm shot out of a cannon. I can't imagine what we were thinking to get married.

Upon reflection, I think it had something to do with great sex. Yes, that was it.

"I knew we could work it out," he said, standing to stretch, reminding me how hard it is to come by a man taller than I am.

I buried myself deeper in my chair, and grumbled to myself, "I knew I should have asked for alimony. Why did I refuse to sign that pre-nup? I would have been better off with at least a pittance."

"Because you're romantic and emotional by nature. It's one of the reasons I fell in love with you." He was feeling guilty. The "L" word was always invoked at such times. He wouldn't give up the damned microwave, but it was something. I felt a little better.

"Look, your show is closed now, isn't it?" I nodded morosely. Like all actors, I knew—just *knew*—no one would ever hire me again for so much as an offstage noise. "What are you doing tonight?"

"Besides my date with Sean Connery?" Might as well pretend to be feisty. "Nothing."

"Great!"

Not having a date with Sean Connery is great? Someday I am definitely going to figure out some way to go out with old Sean, just to be taken seriously for a change and boost my floundering self-image. I date a local TV newsman, but it doesn't seem to make much of an impression except with the two Chinese ladies who live on the third floor of my Upper West Side walk-up. My luck. No one else in New York seems to watch his station, and the two who do don't speak English.

7

"I'm not having sex with you, but dinner would be nice."
Actors always consider an occasion that features free food to
be a reasonable investment of time.

"I have a commitment with Elaine tonight, Vic." He was
looking guilty again, as well he should. I know he needed to
get on with his life, but with a woman that short? She had
brown hair. I couldn't help myself. I glanced at her picture on
his desk. *Dark*-brown hair, and it was straight. I think I hated
her most for that.

"I only do three-ways if you throw in a movie." I couldn't
resist the feeble quip. No wonder his mother hates me. But I
could see by the look in his eyes he was feeling a twinge of
nostalgia for what passes as my wit under duress. I was glad.
Disappointed about the no-food part, but pleased nonetheless.

"No," he said, sounding a little exasperated. "Elaine and
I are hosting a party here tonight. I thought you might like to
come. You might be able to make some connections. There'll
be producers around."

"Will there be food?" I wondered aloud. Producers are
everywhere in New York City.

"Yes. Don't you want to know what it's for?"

"Do I get to dress up?" I hardly ever get to.

"Yes. It's a party for Kendall James—you know, my
soap-opera client. I got him one helluva—"

"May I bring a date?" I was still annoyed, and I have
never been a believer in being annoyed alone.

"A date? Who are you dating now? You date too much."
The obvious hypocrisy must have pinged his flagging conscience. "I worry about you."

"I *have* to date; I'm bereft. I'm on my own at the age of
thirty-nineish. I need to keep my hands busy so I don't do
anything self-destructive." Accenting the last two words, I
looked him squarely in the eye. He flinched. One for my side.

"You used to crochet." Aha, belligerence.

"I used to have electrical appliances." Snide belligerence.
I win.

"Okay, okay, bring a date," Barry conceded. "Just do me a favor and don't make it an actor. I don't want the evening to turn into casting mania."

"You know I don't date actors. Someone has to pay for dinner, and I'm too young for it to be me." I smiled in what I consider to be a moronic Pia Zadora fashion but which Barry has always found appealing. I was beginning to feel sympathetic again. I hate that about me. Anyway, I couldn't rob him of his moment, much as I tried. Especially not when he was looking so damned boyish. How dare forty-two-year-old men look boyish? I do not look in the slightest "girlish." On good days, I can manage stately, for whatever that's worth. "What's the occasion?"

"Oh"—his eyes lit up—"Kendall just signed to star in a new prime-time series shooting on location all over the world. I got some great concessions from the producers." It was so cute. He was so pleased. "I get a percentage of Ken's percentage." He was beaming.

"You already do," I commented.

"Well, sure, but now I get a percentage of *more*. When that first prime-time check arrived, I nearly fainted."

Probably the result of Kendall's blood rushing into Barry's pocket, I thought, but had the good sense not to say. I *did* say, "I still don't understand why Kendall's checks don't go directly to his accountant. She could send you your cut when she pays the rest of the bills." What I wanted to say was, *Elaine sees you often enough, doesn't she, Barry-Boy? She could just drop by with her peek-a-boo undies and a big fat check, couldn't she?* But I didn't.

"Oh," Barry said, "that's Kendall's idea, though it's pretty standard procedure. It's sort of a double-blind system. I take my percentage and send the rest along to Elaine for general accounting and to pay Ken and his wife their allowances. It works. I can't complain." He grinned at me in debonair fashion. "I get my money before anybody else—even Kendall!" Barry laughed at the divine justice.

Why, oh why, did I refuse to sign that pre-nup? That old

unemployed feeling was creeping back up my spine. "What time is the party?"

"Eight. And don't make an entrance; I shouldn't have invited you at all."

Translation: Elaine, who had managed to avoid meeting me for several months, would be really pissed off if I looked too good. Barry was torn. On the one hand, he wouldn't want anyone in his burgeoning entertainment clientele to think he had been married to a toad; on the other hand, he undoubtedly had hopes of getting lucky with short, brown-haired Elaine.

"Would I draw focus?" Transparent innocence. I respected him enough not to try to lull him into a false sense of security, anyway. It served him right. "I'll just grab the coffee machine on the way out." I leaned over the desk and kissed him good-bye. "I love you!"

"I love you, too, God help me," he gallantly mumbled and went back to his manila folder. His head shot suddenly back up. "Don't bring the Italian count, either. Hereditary titles make Americans fidget."

I ducked into the kitchen. "All right, dear." I wasn't actually being amenable; Sergio was still in Rome doing whatever it is that counts do. I spotted the Mr. Coffee on the counter, and checked to make sure the gold forever-and-ever filter was still there.

I had room in my dance bag for the coffee grinder, too. The day was looking up.

Normally, I would have taken the M-104 bus back north, but I'd worked myself into such self-pity over my miserable, unskilled lot, it was going to take a half dozen Dunkin' jelly doughnuts to pull me out of it. I have a strict rule: eating more than four doughnuts means I have to walk for them. I walk a lot for doughnuts. Besides, if I eat them on the street instead of in the apartment, they have no calories. If you don't have to vacuum crumbs up afterward, they don't count.

It was a gorgeous spring day. There's still some air in

10

Manhattan during May, and it was blowing around gently. Carriage horses were happily tethered to their cabs along Central Park South, pointing toward the newly renovated statue at Columbus Circle. The old-fashioned newsstand and Sabrett hot-dog cart catty-corner on Central Park West were doing a banner business from the ambling pedestrians. Across the avenue, on the West Side of Broadway, the shantytown of homeless stood haplessly, ringing the circular sidewalk at the New York Coliseum. The verdant finger of Central Park poked accusingly at the dichotomy.

My hair was frizzing a bit around my forehead, but nothing that couldn't be fixed with some industrial-strength hair spray and electric rollers. I rejected the notion that Barry could be despicable enough to have filched my hot rollers as I turned and entered Dunkin' Donuts.

After twelve years in New York, I still forget not to make assumptions.

There were no jellies at Dunkin' Donuts. There were also no crullers, honey-dip, Boston cream, Bavarian cream, lemon-filled, or glazed. I bought a cinnamon and a plain—which made a peculiar thunking sound when it hit the bottom of the bag. It was definitely time to make the doughnuts. I handed the bag to the odoriferous bum blocking my exit, paper coffee cup from a Greek luncheonette thrust into my face.

"Whaddya want me tido wif dese?" she called after me. I didn't answer. I had no idea. Eating them was out of the question, obviously.

I decided to figure out whom I wanted to take with me to the party as I walked the next eleven blocks. Lincoln Center loomed to my left, the "Mostly Mozart" banner flicking in the breeze. The fountain was turned off—some new economy measure by the mayor, no doubt—but scores of students and tourists sat circling the dry hollow of the pool. I wished I knew a cellist or someone essentially exotic to partner me for the evening, but I didn't. In fact, all the exotic-sounding men I've ever dated always turned out to be pretty much just men (as they say in New Hampshire, "Not much to 'em once you've

11

cleaned 'em"). My choice at the moment was between two basic, but acceptable, examples of the male species.

Brad, the newscaster, had tall and handsome going for him. I passed the spectacular pre-war complex he inhabited— doormen standing at the massive double iron gates, the center garden viciously tormenting those of us whose apartments feature panoramic views of back alleys and brick walls. Television had been good to my Mr. Sinclair. But one can't take an apartment out for the evening, and unfortunately Brad was as undependable as they come. He was always canceling dates over the smallest plane crash or international incident.

I shook off a plastic bag that had somehow attached itself to my foot, and weighed the fact that Dan, the cop, had tall and scary to recommend him. Show-biz types are notoriously skittish around big guys with guns, and it never hurts to be memorable. It was going to be a tough call, the outcome of which ultimately depended on whether I wanted to wear heels. At five feet nine, even a medium heel has me towering at around six feet. Dan outweighed Brad by about fifty pounds (I like that), but Brad was a couple of inches taller. Instead of giving myself a headache, I pulled into the nearest phone booth. Since it was broken, I walked two more blocks to the next broken phone. I was on the corner of my home block before I got a dial tone. By that time, it was a matter of principle, so I wasted the quarter and called my neighbor, Jewel, the person I most trust with my personal life. Since she has been housebound for the last five or ten years, I knew she'd be home.

I have my own keys to Jewel's apartment, as does just about everyone in the neighborhood, so I knocked and let myself in. Jewel LaFleur was reclining, resplendent in a turquoise/purple/hot-pink geometric caftan, looking for all the world like Elizabeth, empress of Russia. Her glorious white foof of hair framed a beatifically grandmotherly face, apple cheeks and clear blue eyes.

You're thinking I made up that name: Jewel LaFleur. I

didn't need to; Jewel did it herself sometime during the embry-onic stage of her career as a stripper—mostly in the forties and fifties. I had to admit it was a fine name for someone who danced naked.

"There's a fresh bottle of Perrier-Jouët in the fridge," she said, pointing toward the kitchen. "Just pop it. You know where the champagne glasses are." I did indeed. "You look like shit, dear; find one of the Lalique goblets for yourself. You'll feel better."

I went, I found, I popped. As I topped off her glass, I said, "I walked up from Fifty-fourth, thinking again."

She crooked an eyebrow and asked, "Did you bring doughnuts?"

It should be mentioned here that Jewel is a fine flotilla of a woman in the feisty prime of her seventy-somethings. I've never thought to ask her weight. I know she'd tell me, though, after about three hundred pounds, the question seems a bit moot. She is the perfect role model for me: all-seeing, all-knowing, all-telling. The only thing Jewel will not, under any circumstances, divulge is her real name. It drives me crazy: absolutely everything else is available to me but her name. I asked her once why she no longer leaves her apartment. She simply said that she's already seen it all, so why walk? Did I mention she's my hero?

"They didn't have anything but stale," I said.

"We could have dunked them in our champagne," she said pragmatically. "Oh, but never mind, darling, how *are* you?" Jewel gifted me with her best motherly look. How she tolerates my endless banal crises only the gods know.

I explained my minor dilemma regarding that night's party and choosing a date. While I was at it, I asked to borrow some good jewelry. She didn't name herself Jewel for nothing. Bracelets, earrings, and necklaces spilled from end tables and hung from paintings. What little I'd owned had been cleaned out in my semi-annual burglary a few months before, but I liked hers better anyway.

"Take the topaz, sweetheart," she said, gesturing to the

baby grand piano stacked with small white boxes. "They flatter redheads and they're big enough that they won't get lost on you. Wear the lovely gold silk outfit that drapes so beautifully, and drag along that newsman person. I know no one watches his show normally, but that desert war had a lot of people tuned in to all sorts of odd news programs, so perhaps someone will accidentally know who he is." Good point. "The only people who might possibly recognize a cop would have felony records." Excellent point. "By the way, is he still on his celibacy kick?"

"It's not celibacy," I argued, "he just doesn't believe in sexual relations with married women. I *am* still married, Jewel. At least technically."

"Where do you find these guys anyway?" Jewel heaved a sigh. Since it was as rhetorical a question as could be, she patted me on the cheek and ordered, "Now run along. Your hair is frizzing a bit, and you want to make a good impression. On your way out, would you take the garbage, please—and grab that paperback on the end table, it's for you; I think Machiavelli is very inspirational during spring divorces."

When Jewel is right, she's right.

CHAPTER
TWO

I told Brad I didn't *care* who was at the U.N. that night.

Brad picked me up in a cab driven by a very pleasant chap from Port-au-Prince who found the difficult task of pointing his vehicle due south and depressing the gas pedal akin to landing the space shuttle. Brad's intense yelling made no impression as we headed north. The windows were all rolled and fixed down, turning my hairdo into coiffure à la Cuisinart. Ultimately, my feverish pleading *en français* got us turned properly. The driver made up for lost time by considerately running every red light for thirty blocks. We arrived at Barry's an hour late anyway.

The party appeared most festive, considering the number of lawyers present. Brad spotted a dissipated older British actor at the far end of the living room with whom he used to carouse, and wandered off to wax nostalgic.

Wham! It hit me.

It was that "old black magic," but it wasn't called love. It was that ugly, pervasive feeling that disaster was brewing—

and not of the "Oops-I-broke-a-nail" type—it was something hovering grotesquely. My eyes scanned the room to try and locate the victim of such malevolent horror. Nothing.

I guess I hate knowing these things even more than I hate going to the dentist, because at the dentist's, at least I have some idea of what to expect—a root canal at worst. I don't know if I wish I were a better psychic receiver so I could efficiently zone in on specifics, or no psychic at all. The ability has saved my butt, and others', on several occasions. Now the bad news is, it's damned near impossible for me to tell the difference between an insight and an educated guess. The emotion was real enough, but was it party nerves? I thought I felt about as panicked as I could. Atypically, I was understating the potential for distress.

"Citrine?" The very short woman with the very brown, straight hair asked, nodding up toward my necklace. The lurch in my gut told me it was Elaine, and that I could, indeed, feel rottener.

It's a good thing short women don't know what great hulking monsters tall women feel like standing next to them— or over them, as the case may be.

"Imperial topaz," I tossed off casually, calculating her inseam measurement at about twenty-two inches, and slumping a bit. She was pretty, I supposed, if you like that incredibly well-turned-out, physically fit type. Well, I could pretend I didn't know who she was, just as well as she could. I wished I'd worn flats, nonetheless, and tried to zero in on the object of my psychic assault.

"Really?" Elaine said, sounding genuinely amazed.

Really, *indeed.*

No doubt about it, my husband's younger-than-me girl-friend was either distracting me from honing in on the particulars of my creepy psychic feeling, or I was jealous. That possibility made me begin to think I'd misjudged the blast of doom completely. Psychic jolts are a lot like radiating tooth pain: often the rotten tooth doesn't turn out to be the one that makes you scream. I thought, perhaps, I was just getting ready for my very own emotional impalement by Elaine's tiny little hand.

"Brazilian, you know." I was sounding like David Niven. It's a reflex I'm trying to learn to stifle.

I wanted height reduction, liposuction, and an Uzi submachine gun. Not necessarily in that order. Where was Brad? Barry conveniently appeared over Elaine's shoulder. I still wished for the Uzi, but less for a supply of ammo clips.

"Elaine, I see you've met Victoria," he "suaved." Victoria? Why not just stamp WASP all over my freckled face?

"Vic. Please just call me Vic," I said, trying to edge away to somewhere where the ceiling was higher. How could I prevent someone else's disaster when I couldn't prevent my own?

"And you can call me Lanie," Elaine said, very much blocking my flight. Now, I realize I could have just stepped over her.

"Lanie," I smiled wanly. The woman had a nickname like a turnpike. This wasn't going to be as easy as I'd hoped. Even so, the room was full to the built-in bookcases with television contacts. I reassured myself that I was just crazy and hadn't gotten a true precognitive zap. Besides, whoever said business parties are supposed to be fun?

"Isn't this *fun?*" asked Barry.

"It certainly *is,*" agreed Lanie.

"I don't know," I said, "I haven't started drinking yet." Maybe I'd just sensed Lanie was going to be as intimidating to me as she was. I gave up trying to analyze my feeling.

"Well, Vickie, let me get on that waiter!" Lanie offered with the kind of enthusiasm that only the profoundly cute can seem to muster.

"Vic," I said feebly, "no *i-e.*"

It is my opinion that there is an age at which all people should be forced by law to drop *i*'s, *y*'s, and/or *i-e*'s from their names, but that's probably because I was never "cute," and thus didn't get a nickname until I made up my own.

Without taking a beat, Lanie said, "Now, where is that waiter? I'll take care of it, Bear." She dipped like a dancer, and wove her way into the crowd. I kicked off my heels. I didn't want to find myself plowing through perfect strangers like an enormous icebreaker.

"Bare? How suggestive." Not much of a conversation piece, but I was stressed. Diminutives of all varieties were getting on my nerves. Valiantly, I put the heels back on.

"Bear. B-E-A-R."

"Cute."

"Don't be bitchy, Vic." Barry likes conflict, actually. I think it's one of the reasons he's such a good lawyer. It makes him feel needed. "By any chance, I don't suppose you brought your tarot deck?"

"I did not," I answered—a bit shrilly, I think.

During professional dry periods—of which there have been more than three, but less than a million—I have been known to tell fortunes at the parties of the rich and famous. I'm good at it, and I loathe doing it. After a lot of trouble, I finally had managed to pretty much price myself out of the market. It was one of the few things Barry respected about me: the fee, and that—from time to time, out of the blue—I actually do know what people are thinking. If the talent were more dependable, I'd play the stock market. Unfortunately, like a cat, it just comes and goes of its own will.

"I *am* a guest," I reminded him with false dignity.

"Well, I just thought, you know, if the party slows down too much . . . well, I don't have to tell you how much people love that garbage."

"I could go home and get them." His eyes lit up. "I charge two hundred the first hour and one fifty for each after." I figured this party would be good for at least four hours, and that would buy me a pretty damned good microwave. With a carousel. Still, even unpaid, the creepy feelings were with me, and I couldn't help but ask my almost-ex, "Is there someone here who's sick? Or an accident-prone sky diver or something?"

He ignored me, but without malice. "I suggest you go over and mingle in that group." He indicated the crowd in the farthest corner, featuring my disappearing date. "Sal Steinbeck, the head writer of the new series, is there. He's the heavy-set, middle-aged guy."

"I think he's cute—in a kind of 'accountant to the mob' sort of way," I offered, hoping to torture Barry just a little bit.

"Is there a man alive you *don't* think is sexy?"

Direct hit. "I didn't say he was sexy, Barry. I said 'cute.' " Though I was, indeed, *thinking* sexy, in a sort of worked-his-way-up fashion. Barry let the matter drop.

"Sure." Barry craned slightly and nodded at Sal Steinbeck's side. "And the blonde to his right is Lissa Stevens, Kendall's love interest on 'Raging Passions.' God, she's gorgeous. If she were my leading lady, I'd think twice about going to prime time."

Another direct hit for the ex-husband's side. I retaliated. "She *is* your type: eyes like the sky, brain like a cumulonimbus."

"A *what?*"

I weighed exactly how jealous and hateful I was feeling. Mr. Webster defines a cumulonimbus as an "extremely dense, vertically developed cumulus with a relatively hazy outline and a glaciated top . . ." Good breeding won out. "It's a cloud," I explained.

"Oh." He let it go, and continued, "And in the center is—jeez, that's Brad Sinclair. I didn't know we'd invited *press.*" Barry straightened his power tie. It was like turning on a light.

One point for my side. Jewel had made the right dating decision for me. These small moments of petty revenge can make life worth living.

Barry made the connection and glared at me. "You *didn't,*" he growled under his breath.

I smiled smugly and plowed through the crowd to my date—toward whom I was now feeling extremely affectionate.

Brad had just finished telling one of those newsroom jokes, fraught with pithy issues, famous names, death, dismemberment, and toiletries. I'm told that doctors tell the same sort of jokes. I know cops do. They amuse me inordinately, but then I am notoriously shallow. Apparently, so are head writers, soap-opera divas, and casting directors because they were all laughing uproariously. I tucked myself neatly under Brad's arm. I didn't have to slump much.

A medium-sized, stocky brunette in glasses, wearing a loud Hawaiian shirt recklessly jammed into an oversized pair of khakis, frowned. "Do I know you?" she asked.

I decided not to start out witty.

"No."

Brad briefly paused for the clever follow-up he reasonably expected me to make, and then came up with his own segue. "I'm going to find something to drink. Pernod for you, Vic?"

"Bourbon, rocks," I said.

When threatened by new situations, I regress to my lobster-fisherman roots: another reflex that could use stifling.

The brunette continued, lowering her red pagoda glasses and peering over the top at me. "I'm sure I saw you a few years ago. *Chorus Line?* Of course!" This woman was not going to let go of this.

You see, apparently I look as though I ought to be someone even though I'm not. I accept it because it happens so often, but it's a constant—and stinging—reminder that I haven't done very well: looking at faces fallen with disappointment over my admitted unknownness. I used to give up and say, "Perhaps *Brideshead Revisited,*" because, when pressed, most people won't admit they never watch public television. It's a horrible lie, but they're happy, and I'm off the hook.

"You're probably thinking of Donna McKechnie." I grimaced. "I'm Victoria 'I don't dance, don't ask me' Bowering."

"That's right!" the woman said, shifting her weight from one leg to the other. "Hi, I'm Olive Abedin."

I didn't know whether she meant That's right, Donna McKechnie or That's right, I'm me. And if I am me, had she ever seen me work? This sort of quandary is one of the reasons actors tend to be unstable emotionally. Perhaps it showed on my face, because the man on my right, whom Barry had identified as Sal Steinbeck, jumped into the fray.

"I'm Sal, headwriter for Kendall's new series, 'SPA!' Nice to meetcha! This is Lissa."

Lissa moved forward and shook my hand, smiling as though she meant it. Hell, I can admit it, I liked her immediately, even though she was younger and, well, all right, *gorgeous.*

"You're Barry Laskin's wife, aren't you?" Lissa asked, not intending to make my stomach lurch.

"Ex," I corrected, as blasé as William Buckley.

"Really?" the burly headwriter/producer asked, oozing subtext. "Olive here does all my casting. You're an actress, right?"

"Right." I thought it showed more than that. Now more pressure: remembering names. I *really* needed some work. Luckily, the work I wanted so badly had trained me for short-term memorization. Any actor worth her salt knows the trick. Association. Olive was easy, since she had kindly dressed herself in green. The headwriter was more complicated, so I had to stretch. He was standing with Olive; an olive is a fruit; a grape is a fruit and the same color almost as a ripe olive; who wrote *Grapes of Wrath?* Steinbeck! Producers and headwriters make the hard decisions; who was the most notable of decision-makers? Solomon! *A* Solomon; *a* instead of *o!* Voilà—Sal, not Sol. Sal Steinbeck! Trust me, it sounds more complex than it is.

"I also do 'Raging Passions,' " Olive said, pulling at her green trousers, which were hiking up toward her green belt. "I was hoping to find a soap-opera stud-type here tonight, actually. It's going to be hard to replace Kendall."

"Wish I could help." And I did. The concept of a sex-change operation is not all that daunting to an unemployed actor, after all. But before volunteering prematurely to go under the knife, I said, "I thought 'SPA!' was already cast."

"Oh, it is, for the most part, but we're always looking," said Sal. He certainly was. At me, anyway. I was glad I wore the gold silk. It's very short and, as Jewel is constantly reminding me, the legs are the last thing to go. Sal reached in his pocket and pulled out a wildly vulgar "new money" gold case. "Here's my card. Give me a call. Maybe something will come up."

Okay, so I wasn't imagining things. Sometimes it's difficult for me to tell.

"You know," Olive said, "I'm looking for extras right now for the massacre-in-Scotland scenes shooting this week on 'Raging Passions.' " She sipped intently at her drink while inspecting my arms. "Are those real freckles?"

You're not going to believe this, but this was not the first time I've been asked that question. It's hard to bite down sarcasm under those circumstances, but I did.

"Yes."

"You have quite a few, don't you?" she continued.

How do you answer something like that?

"Yes," I responded, rapier-like.

"Look, I could use a barmaid. Most of the present cast gets killed in a pub in Glasgow. Think you can look Scottish for a day or two?"

"Of course she can!" Lissa helped out. Bless her.

"Sure." An honest assertion from me for a change, inasmuch as my grandfather was born and raised in Angus, though—I admit it—I was shamelessly prepared to convince her I could be African by show time. (I still needed three weeks to qualify for unemployment.) I decided to be nicer to Barry for the rest of the evening.

"Great," Olive enthused. "Report at the studio at seven A.M. Don't worry about costume pieces, unless you have something Scottish and barmaidy hanging in the closet. By any chance, do you know how to tend bar?"

Now that's like asking a cowboy if he can ride.

"Like a pro," I said. No need to bore everyone with my tales of months spent slinging brandy Alexanders. It was yet

22

another truth told in an effort to bag some work, but she didn't believe me anyway. No doubt she'd been in the business for a while, listening to untold numbers of aspiring stars lie through their capped teeth.

"Doesn't matter. You probably won't have to do anything technical. Looking ethnic is all that really matters." She smiled in reassurance.

Ethnic? I smiled back. I've always wanted to be ethnic.

"Sorry it doesn't pay more," Olive apologized. "I know how hard it is to get along on alimony."

"I'm not actually getting alimony."

"Interim support, whatever," Olive amended.

Of course, I was getting neither. I thought it would prolong my dependence on Barry. Or was that just what Barry thought? In any event, I was too embarrassed to continue. Lissa patted my arm, looking genuinely pleased about having me around the set for a day or two.

"Great!" Lissa exclaimed. "I thought I was going to be bored spitless tomorrow." Any woman who can use the word "spit" is aces in my book.

Sal waved into the mob. Kendall James was weaving his way confidently toward us. As he got closer, Sal pronounced, "There he is! There's our star!" Headwriters, like actors, talk with a lot of exclamation points. It's one of the reasons our parents are always telling us "keep it down, for heaven's sake."

Kendall accepted the hugs and backclaps with exuberance. No doubt about it, this was his party. He looked fit, too, as though he'd been working out, and somehow had managed to get a golden tan in New York City. Probably a tanning booth at the gym. It set off his signature green eyes beautifully.

I hadn't seen Kendall in more than a year, and that had been at one of Barry's obligatory client-relationship dinners during the last gasp of our marriage. Since I had been cooking, and as usual had gotten dreadfully carried away with my own culinary imaginings, I'd spent most of the time in the kitchen. Kendall's wife, Frances, had wandered in periodically to make certain I hadn't fallen into the garbage disposal, but Kendall and Barry stayed glued to the table or a computer game, so we didn't have much of a chance to talk. There was too much lemon in the hollandaise, and I had to read Frances's cards twice. Otherwise, the night was another one of those transitory successes.

Kendall held out his arms. "Sal! Olive!"

I wondered if I'd spent so much time in the kitchen that Kendall didn't recognize me. It was an unfounded neurosis.

"Vic!" Kendall said, hugging me, as actors are wont to do. Even though he was wearing cowboy boots, he still had to tippy-toe a bit. His hands were cold.

I hugged back. "Hi, Ken, I guess I don't have to ask you how things are going."

"Nope, I'm great!" he answered, kissing Lissa on the cheek. "Glad you could make it," he added while bussing Olive's cheek. "I was afraid that . . . well, anyway, are you doing a show now?"

There it was, the standard polite inquiry, intimating his faith that I was capable of getting a show.

"Just closed," I gave the standard response, hoping I looked relieved to have the horrific pressure of a regular paycheck lifted from my artistic back. "Olive's given me some day work on 'RP,' though. I'll see you tomorrow."

Soap operas are always referred to by their initials: "Y&R," "OLTL," "DOOL," "GH," "ATWT." I don't know why, I just know if you don't do it, people think you just got in from Franconia Notch, which is pretty near to where I'd come from fifteen years before. "Live Free or Die," was the New Hampshirite creed—and license plate—along with this New Hampshirite's motto, "Initial Caps or Look Stupid and Starve."

"Great!" Kendall was being more effusive than usual. Well, why not?

I noticed that his California-blond hair was a bit longer in back than his soap-opera character of a brilliant surgeon would have worn it. But then, he knew his Dr. Carrollton was

24

going to be killed off this week, so there was no need to maintain surgical hair. I also noticed that he looked a little thin for prime time.

For some unknown reason, actors are always said to have "looks." Mine, unfortunately, is a "stage" look, every feature unsubtle. The kind of face that screams on a monitor. Kendall had definitive "daytime" looks: for lack of a better word, modelish. Videotape, which is the medium in which soap operas are shot, is grotesquely unkind to humans. Film, used in more expensive prime time and movies, forgives much more. I'd always liked Kendall James, but I couldn't shake the impression that he was too pretty for nighttime viewing somehow. A martini appeared in my hand. Brad drinks martinis.

I nodded pleasantly to him and stole a drag off his cigarette. Actually, the gin tasted good. He kissed me emphatically, which is how he does it, and he tasted good, too. I wondered where he'd gotten the buffalo chicken wings, and looked around the room for a buffet table.

"Frances and I just bought a place in California, Vic. Let me give you the number, in case you get out to the coast," Kendall offered. He dug in his pockets. "I had cards printed. I know they're here somewhere." He pulled out his wallet and some credit-card receipts. Looking puzzled, he balanced them between his teeth and continued his search. He came up with a pen and change purse, which he tucked in his mouth to the right of the wallet.

"Watch it, Ken," said Sal. "You don't want to ruin that million-dollar smile now that the pilot is in the can."

Lissa smiled. "He's always doing that." She sipped her drink. "Makeup is always after him because of ink stains around his mouth from the spitty scripts." She wiped a smudge from Kendall's upper lip.

Kendall looked fondly abashed, and removed the articles from his mouth. I noticed teeth marks in all the items. Obviously, Kendall didn't worry much about germs. He said, "Barry can give it to you, can't he?"

I nodded.

25

"Well, congratulations," Brad said to Kendall. "Word is, the new show is a shoo-in for an Emmy." I grabbed the cigarette from his hand before he could put it out. "I don't hear that often."

"Bank on it," Sal asserted as his fingers slid down my back. "There's never been a premise like 'SPA!' on network television," he continued, as did his hand. "Imagine, a bionic health instructor with the ability to transport himself anywhere in the world through just the power of his mind!"

Unkindly, I thought that, kissing fifty, Kendall looked a little long in the tooth for that sort of gymnastic feat, no matter how many hours he put in pumping iron. When I get hungry, I get unkind.

"Maybe he should run for mayor," Brad quipped. "There are certain persons who take prolonged commercial air travel awfully personally."

There was just a minor pause in the group's effervescence. Lissa graced me with an understanding look.

"Go figure," Steinbeck pronounced, obviously befuddled by the jab.

"Right!" Kendall assisted innocently, having reorganized his pockets.

Sal rallied. "Very funny, Sinclair. Really. Anyway, unlike the mayor, we've got a hit!" He wrapped a nicely hirsute arm around Kendall's shoulder and shook it firmly. Twice.

I edged myself slightly backward and whispered in Brad's ear, "Where's the food?" He pointed back toward the dining room and threw down the dregs of his drink.

"Could you get me another martini while you're at it? Beefeater." At that, he turned back to the group. I didn't much care. I was starving. As usual.

"Vic!" Kendall's wife, Frances James, blocked my escape route in search of sustenance. She'd been drinking. I could smell Jack Daniel's as she hugged me. Well, at least I could have my bourbon, after all. I mentioned my desire to the apparently hearing-impaired waiter passing through.

"Frances!" I looked down upon a veritable sea of sequins. Frances didn't usually fuss with herself—I usually remembered *her* name by thinking "James Franciscus, only backward and not as long"—so I made a point to compliment her. She flushed slightly, pleased. She, too, looked as though she'd been exercising and sunning. Most people are too busy looking at Kendall to pay Frances, who leans to the plain side, much notice. If they had that night, they would have seen tiny red marks that indicated a recent face-lift. I was glad she'd decided to bloom a little.

"Oh, did you bring your tarot cards? Please say you did. I have a thousand questions to ask you!" she cajoled. I fervently hoped no one caught the reference.

"You tell fortunes?" asked Sal immediately.

Before I could say no and get to a shrimp ball, Frances chimed in, "She's wonderful. Wonderful!"

You should know that there is almost nothing that I will not do to avoid telling fortunes at parties at which I am a guest. No matter how "skeptical," there is not a person alive who won't want his or her fortune told. "Sorry. Didn't bring the cards," I apologized.

I wasn't sorry at all, naturally. If I got started, by the end of the evening, after everyone else had left, I would still be staring, stupefied, into the palms of the catering staff.

"Then read my *palm!*" Frances wheedled.

She then proceeded to regale the assembled with charmingly inflated stories of my fabulous psychic powers. My stomach growled. Sal launched into a monologue about a movie of the week he'd written on that very subject. Even Kendall started to beg for a reading. Terrific. I was trapped in a clump of believers. Where was my bourbon?

"Forget it," said Brad. "She won't tell *my* fortune. I have to call Dial a Psychic." Even my *date* was nagging.

"Sorry, guys, I'm just not very good with people I know." Baleful eyes pleaded. "You see, I want everything to turn out perfectly for my friends, and only a totally objective reading is worth anything." I shrugged with thoughtful humility, and managed to get myself somewhat extricated and on a path to the food.

"You don't really know me," shot Brad, petulantly, for the thousandth time.

Brad is frighteningly superstitious for a professional news reporter. That, coupled with the requisite aggressiveness, can be enormously irritating.

"No, who *could* truly understand anyone so complex?" I sniped. That brought a laugh from all but Brad.

"You're *giving* me a complex," he sulked.

Trapped like a rat, I countered, "I hope not, darling. But you must understand, I most especially don't make predictions for men I'm having sex with." I thought that was a terrific exit line, and moved off while it was appreciated. Within one yard, Sal was behind me.

"Then you should read my palm tonight," he said, meaningfully accentuating the time frame.

"What?" I extricated myself. "And lessen the anticipation?"

Little did I know how much there was to look forward to.

By the time I got to the buffet, it looked like a filleted carp: all bones and wide eyes. I believe I sighed.

"I got the last shrimp ball. Want it?" A masculine hand proffered a very sad-looking ovoid object. I popped it in my mouth immediately. Nonetheless, I figured I'd better check out the general health profile of my benefactor before swallowing the suspicious foodstuff.

He was mid-sixties, I judged—gray thinning hair, barrel chest, and hands like hams: true stage-manager material. He didn't appear the slightest bit contagious, so I chewed thankfully.

"I don't suppose you know where there's some bourbon?" I asked.

"Follow me." He led the way into the kitchen. "These West Side parties always hide the good stuff under the sink until after everyone leaves. Wow!" the man enthused when he saw the dozens of liquor bottles. "This is some stash!" He went to the refrigerator, put some ice cubes in a glass, and poured two or three fingers of brand-name booze. Then he topped off his own. *"Salut!"*

"Bless you." I took a deep sip and leaned heavily against the sink. Barry had had a bottled-water machine installed in the few hours since I'd repossessed my coffee machine—the empty space had already been plugged with a cappuccino maker *and* a homemade-bread machine. I was too grateful for the cheese my hero had scrounged out of the vegetable bin to be bitter.

"You an actress?" the stage manager/godsend asked.

"How could you tell?" I munched.

"You're eating American cheese. New Yorkers with real jobs wouldn't touch the stuff." He leaned on the sink, next to me. "My name's Jack," he said, "Jack Metelenis," taking a sip of his drink. "I don't know what I'm doing here. And you're . . .?"

"Vic Bowering. I don't know what I'm doing here either." We clinked glasses. Jack, I thought, jack cheese! I guessed I could remember that. "I used to be married to the host and I've already gotten day work on a soap for tomorrow, so I suppose I might as well go home now."

" 'RP'?" Jack asked.

"What else?"

"Well, you're in luck. I'll be your director du jour." So much for my fabulous intuitive powers. "I guess that makes both of us beside the point, doesn't it?" He opened the refrigerator again and pulled out an apple. He chewed thoughtfully and offered me a bite. I took it. "After we kill off Kendall at the end of the week, the four audience members we have left will defect. He's the only cast member with a following anymore, and now he's leaving."

"It can't be that bad," I offered.

He toasted me with the apple core, and walked toward the door. "See you on unemployment!"

I was ready to go home to my coffee machine, but, like so

many of life's little pleasures, it was not to be. Jack had stopped cold in the doorway. I peered over his shoulder to see what had frozen him, and spotted another "RP" cast member striding purposefully into the crowded living room. I recognized him immediately as David Ogden; heartthrob of the prepubescent: all chiseled features, pumped-up muscles, and dark eyes. Conversation dropped to a murmur, and tight clusters of guests parted, allowing him a beeline to where Kendall was still ensconced in the corner with Olive, Brad, and Sal.

For a moment, I thought I was the only person present who didn't have a clue as to what was happening. Then Barry's voice cut through as he regaled the "RP" ingenue, Lissa Stevens, who had moved away to the center of the room, with stories of his junior class play, unmindful of the drama that was playing itself out in his own living room. Count on Barry to be oblivious. Lissa's crystalline-blue eyes were locked on Ogden. She handed Barry her glass and pursued David like a mother chasing a recalcitrant child into a dangerous intersection.

"Is something happening?" I asked Jack, who was blocking my full view of the action. If that's what it was.

Without averting his eyes from Ogden, he answered tiredly, "God, I hope not."

The crowd was trying very hard to seem uninterested, while maintaining enough of a hush that not a word from the young actor would be missed. Frances marked his approach with flinty eyes I'd not noticed before. Kendall, alone, looked unaffected. When Ogden reached him, he smiled hugely. I couldn't make out the words, but I would have sworn that Kendall was delighted by the other man's surprise guest appearance. Frances, on the other hand, displayed the kind of expression most women save for roach infestations: phobic irrationality.

"I swear," Jack commented more to himself than to me, "the only thing more like a soap opera *than* a soap opera is a soap-opera-cast party."

I turned to Jack, all raised eyebrows. I'll admit it, I'm one of those insatiable voyeurs. I'm never completely happy unless I know precisely everything. But before I had the chance to pump Jack for clarifying information, Frances's voice cut through the apartment.

"What are you doing here?" she slurred at Ogden. "I told you not to come! What is the matter with you?"

I squeezed myself into the six inches available next to Jack in the doorway. Lissa had made it to Frances's side and was whispering something to David Ogden while holding Frances's arm. He ignored her and said something to Kendall. It must have been juicy, because Frances started screeching as if she'd been knifed. She shoved Lissa sharply away.

Jack moved out of the doorway and in the direction of the disturbance. I followed in his wake figuring that, being as big as I am, I might be able to do something with Frances. As it turned out, it wasn't necessary.

Lissa grabbed David by the arm and literally dragged him through the spectators and out the door. As he grazed by me, I got the distinct impression that he'd been doing a little recreational pharmaceutica—probably grass. Kendall trailed behind his two co-stars, seeming very much in possession of himself. Very odd, even to me.

Frances was sniffling into Sal's broad shoulder, while Brad was standing journalistically, one eyebrow raised.

"How dare he," Frances wailed. Sal winked at me over her hunched back. "I hate him." She raised her face and turned in the direction of the open door. Kendall walked through it and back into the room as casually as he'd left. When she saw her husband, Frances's voice became flat. "Would you drop me at home, Sal? I'm not feeling very well." With that, she marched out of the party, nearly knocking Kendall into the foyer wall. Sal shrugged, winked provocatively once again, and followed. I shuttled over to Brad's corner and took another drag of his cigarette.

"What was that all about?" I asked.

"Not much," Brad answered.

31

"It certainly sounded like 'much.' What kind of a newsman are you, anyway?"

"A tired one." Brad held up my arm to glance at my phony Rolex, purchased at a sidewalk stall on Fourteenth Street for ten dollars. "I have to be at a state-of-the-city address first thing tomorrow morning," he said, placing his arm around my waist and moving toward the exit door. "Let's go home and neck."

So much for his journalistic curiosity.

I tried to get Barry's attention to wave good-bye, but he was entranced by Elaine at the moment. I would have had more success establishing eye contact with a SCUD missile.

It was okay; it didn't bother me a bit.

I didn't care.

Really.

CHAPTER
THREE

One of the best things about Brad is his photographic memory. He never needs cue cards or TelePrompTers. When you see him on the screen, standing amid body bags and flames, talking, that's precisely what he's doing. No notes or tape recorders, just his fabulous memory and performing union voice.

"That's it? That's all he said?" I took a sip of chocolate milk, careful not to spill on my best white eyelet sheets.

"That's it. 'Have you got a minute, Ken?' That's all." He took a drag off my cigarette that time. "Do you have any Perrier?"

"Are you kidding? Have some cholesterol, it'll do you good." I offered him my glass. "I'm down to the good syrupy part. You can share it; that's how inclined I am toward you at the moment." He kissed my proffered mouth without taking a beat. Brad is also a hugger. I like that.

"No, thanks," he said. "That stuff'll kill you." He walked over to the cherry veneer bureau and got his cigarettes. When he lit the match, he was briefly illuminated in the tall thin gilt mirror propped behind a vase of pink roses on the bureau surface. Whenever I manage to stay up late enough for his local talk show, that's how I see him: naked and partially illuminated. Believe me, it makes a lot of redundant talk about New York City's impending fiscal disaster much more palatable. "I'm about to fall asleep." He yawned.

"Your pants are in the living room." I yawned too. Extras don't get makeup magic, so I was going to have to be getting up in about another hour and a half. Aargh.

"Oh, come on, Vic, I'm an old man. Let me spend the night. What are you afraid of?"

"That you will be even *lovelier* first thing in the morning," I demurred.

I don't sleep with men, even if we're having sex. There are a lot of reasons for this. For one, if he spends the night, exactly when does the date end? Before coffee? After? Do I get lunch? For another, what if I liked it? What if I stopped being able to sleep well without him? And last, what if he were to wake up wanting sex before I've brushed my teeth or gone to the bathroom? *Worst* of all, what if he discovered the truth: that I loathe waking up alone?

"Get dressed." I pointed him toward the long peach-painted hall. "We both have early mornings, and you're not as young as I look."

He cupped my chin in his hands. "Do you have any idea how beautiful you are?" He kissed me much more softly than is his custom, and ran a finger over my bottom lip. Rather irritably, he added, "Never in my life have I met a woman who made me this crazy." He kissed me again, Brad-style, bruised lips and tangled hair.

"Really, Brad," I said as I disengaged myself, somewhat discomfited by the unexpected sentiment, "you're going to have to get around more."

I'm not going to kid you here. Brad has been unfoundedly hinky for me since moment one. I think he likes me well enough. I make him laugh quite a bit. But, for the most part,

34

it's some bizarre, hyperglandular physical thing, and I can't for the life of me figure out why. I'm not a Gorgon, mind you, but my agent isn't submitting me for any sex-goddess roles, either. I've given it a lot of thought, and decided it has something to do with a fundamental slatternly quality I radiate: oversized lips, and hair that is reminiscent of an unmade bed. In Manhattan, I've met bus drivers who are prettier. Go figure.

Brad shook me mildly, irritated again, and stalked off to retrieve the path of clothing. "You are a pain in the ass."

"Thank you." I threw on a short white silk kimono.

Pants on, he rolled Slasher, my cat, over from where he was curled up on the sofa and dug out one warm sock from beneath the animal's belly. "There are women who would love to sleep with me," he said. "I have a fan club, you know."

"Edna Sandberg, in Long Island City. I remember."

"Besides her." He was on his knees, running his hand under the sofa, looking for his other sock. I walked into my hall storage closet to the litter box, retrieved the sock, shook off the clay pebbles, and handed it to him.

"Like who?" I asked.

"Women without cats," he said, dangling the sock from one hand. "Why does Slasher do that?"

"He likes you." I knew Brad was right about the women waiting in the wings. I chose not to think too much about it. We were both free. Still, without wanting to, I knew there was one woman he saw often. I knew it from that woman-place down in the pit of my stomach—or maybe that fortune-teller place, very nearby. And I knew she was older than me, had marketable skills—and, most disheartening of all—was smarter. Certainly when it came to men.

Brad grunted and sat down to put on the sock. "I think he's a fag," he said, pushing Slasher out of his lap.

"He is *not*. He's just fixed. His orientation is strictly normal." I picked up Slasher and let him bite my nose.

"Not the damn cat. Ogden. Queer as a kipper, unless I

35

miss my guess." He started buttoning his shirt. "Have you seen my cuff links?"

I found one on the kitchen floor, retrieved the other from the bathroom where it had gotten kicked, and handed them to him. "Think so? Usually I can tell." I sat down in my crewel-embroidered wing chair. Slasher joined me and crawled under my kimono. He fell asleep and started snoring instantly.

"Might explain Frances's reaction," Brad offered.

"You mean Ogden and *Kendall?*" I leaned forward. Slasher snorted once and rolled over inside my robe.

"Just a thought." He slipped on his shoes. "Oh, don't look so surprised. How many musicals have you done, anyway?"

I guess I was tired, but the thought still surprised me. It had never even occurred to me that Kendall might be a switch hitter. Yet Brad might be right. I'd done ten weeks on the road in *Best Little Whorehouse in Texas,* where my performance as Miss Mona had been the butchest thing onstage. Even my Sheriff Ed Earl had swung both ways—mostly not mine.

"I'll ask around tomorrow on the set," I said, wrapping my arms over his shoulders. "Wouldn't that be fun if I never suspected? I get so tired of being jaded." I kissed him sweetly. "I'm sorry I make you crazy." I really was.

He ignored me. "And Olive's a lesbian, you know."

"I knew that." Which was interesting, since I usually have more trouble identifying gay women.

"I'll call you tomorrow," he said. The candy-store brass bell that hung over the door jingled as he closed it behind him.

Of course he wouldn't call the next day. Al Sharpton would have some injustice to denounce, and Brad would be sent out to stand in the middle of a hostile confrontation in some far-flung borough like Far Rockaway, Queens. Or it would be a plane crash, or there'd be a fire, or Donald Trump would be refusing to comment on something. I was accustomed to it. And happily, I was darned excited about getting day work on "RP."

My last soap had been three or four years before. I only

36

got one day because my red hair had strobed under the lights and stolen focus from the lead characters during the pivotal dinner-in-a-restaurant scene.

I reminded myself that pubs are dark, and extra pay scale was up to $182 a day. Only two more weeks to qualify for unemployment.

And what lovely rumors to explore.

As usual, I had no idea.

CHAPTER
FOUR

My flamingo alarm clock went off exactly as set, approximately seven and one half hours shy of allowing me a decent night's sleep. Slasher continued snoring contentedly under the sheets as I disentangled my legs from around his body. He made quite a luxuriant lump in the straightened, but not tucked in, bed. I knew he'd come to, famished, about the moment I tried to get out the door, and I didn't want him trapped beneath the eyelet percale.

I opened the sliding closet door to figure out what to wear to the set, but found the entire proposition of deciding anything at all beyond my dawn capabilities, and groped my way to the kitchen—and my coffee machine. It was set to brew, so I just punched the button and dropped myself into the bathtub. Women with frizzy hair don't take showers, if they can help it. When I'd toweled off, I realized I'd forgotten to plug in the coffee machine. That accomplished, I went back to the bedroom, sat on the edge of the bed and stared stupidly into the closet until the coffee was brewed. Morning is not my most sparkling time of the day.

The TV was tuned to the Fox Network morning show. A tall Australian chap was knocking on strangers' doors somewhere in Queens and asking to come in and cook them breakfast. I put on my makeup as doors were slammed in his face, wishing the Aussie weren't married. Very few guys are tall enough for me to waltz with. Face on, I stared again into the black hole of my wardrobe. Slasher woke up, looking more disheveled than I did, so I went back to the kitchen and fed him before he started nagging. He, however, had opted for an early-morning nap.

By that time, I had exactly twenty-three minutes to get dressed and trundle myself to the studio, so I grabbed the definitive actress uniform: black spandex leggings and black cotton tunic top with oversized belt. After all, dressing indecisive actors is what the union wardrobe department gets paid for. A quick look in the mirror next to the door informed me that my hair was a nightmare. I looked as if I were wearing Lassie.

There was no time to wait for a bus, so I speed-walked the fifteen blocks to the studio, muscling through herd after herd of early-morning amblers. At every subway entrance along the way I was swallowed up into the voracious maw of hundreds of jostling New Yorkers anxious to make their escape from the claustrophobic underground holding tanks. Thank heavens for the time I could make up in the open stretches with my long legs. Still, I was perspiring as I presented myself to the uniformed guard behind the front desk at the network. He looked up briefly to see if I was anyone. As a pro, he knew immediately that I wasn't, and mumbled, "Sign in, fifth floor. Wardrobe on seven." Apparently, he'd seen quite a few Scottish-looking actors already. I dashed through the metal detector and into—wonder of wonders—an available elevator. I punched the button for five, and "door close" simultaneously. Two minutes to spare.

"Hold the elevator!"

One of the most annoying things about being raised in a small New Hampshire town is that manners get hammered into you from birth. My first reaction upon being awakened by phone in the middle of the night by a drunken ex-boyfriend is to apologize for having fallen asleep. I accept that I can't seem to get over my upbringing, but New York is not the place to be walking around with this kind of disability. I hit the "door open" button before I could help myself.

"Hold it!"

I was holding, damn it. My time window was rapidly disintegrating. What was taking this bozo so long? Holding my finger on the "door open" button, I poked my head around the elevator doors. Brad was hobbling slowly toward me.

"Vic!" He didn't speed up a microsecond.

"Brad, for God's sake, I'm late," I said. "Shake it."

Just as he entered the elevator, another person yelled from the reception desk, "Hold the elevator!"

I punched the "door close" button with malice aforethought. Brad leaned over to nuzzle. I hit the twelfth floor, where his office was located, and said, "I hate you."

"You do not," he answered. "Did you hit twelve?" Seeing I had, he went back to nuzzling. I've never figured out what it is about men and elevators. Some low-grade mile-high-club syndrome, no doubt.

"What's wrong with your leg?" I asked.

"Old skiing injury. How about a kiss?"

"No. You've made me late. I'll get fired, and starve to death subsisting in some discarded refrigerator box in Times Square." I kissed him good-bye as the doors opened on my floor. "I hate you."

Fortunately for me, there was a sign marked in felt-tip pen with an arrow pointing toward the extras' dressing area. I careened around the corner and into a room filled to the ventilating shaft with Scottish-looking people. I gave my name to the monitor and collapsed into a folding chair, wanting a cigarette very badly. Of course it wasn't allowed.

The monitor said, "Wardrobe will be up in a minute or two," and left.

40

A big red-haired man with muscles and a fascinating tattoo was asleep on the floor. Two red-haired ingenues were playing cards in the corner. All other redheads were reading paperbacks or *Backstage,* the New York show-business-casting weekly. I wondered if the innocent populace of Scotland had any idea of what this casting director's concept of their constituency was.

"Vic?" I looked up to see Lissa Stevens standing in the entryway. "I'm Lissa, remember? We met at Barry's party last night." I knew that, but was pleased she remembered. "Come and sit with me in my dressing room; I need a cigarette." Bless her and all the blondes in the world.

Yes, I know I should quit smoking, and I will. Honest. It's just that I forget to do it first thing in the morning, and I'm just *sure* that I read somewhere that that's when quitting should occur. I wouldn't want to risk getting the bends or anything.

Lissa's dressing room was the usual—nothing like you see in a Lauren Bacall movie—just a cube about six by eight feet with two folding chairs and a long makeup shelf in front of a garishly lit mirror. The picture was complete with the industrial carpet in a 1960s burnt orange, and boxes piled in a corner used for storage.

"I really should quit," Lissa said, lighting up her cigarette. "Coffee?" She poured from a thermos. "I hope black is all right. I'm dieting, as usual." I said it was perfect and that I was certain she would go to heaven. I settled into the unoccupied folding chair. "That was quite a party, wasn't it?" Lissa asked rhetorically. I agreed rhetorically that it was. "What happened after David and I left?" she inquired casually.

Aha. It was not the pleasure of my scintillating wit that Lissa wanted. I wasn't hurt. Gossiping is a favorite sport in theater: it updates constantly and doesn't cost a penny.

"Not much interesting," I said, gratefully exhaling smoke. "Frances cried a little more, and Sal Steinbeck took her home. I didn't get to find out anything juicy. Do you know what it was about?"

"Sort of," Lissa said vaguely. "David wasn't talking much, either. Very frustrating. I was hoping to get the whole poop from him today, but he called in sick. More coffee?"

"Thanks." I held out my Styro cup. "Brad seems to think that David Ogden is a little light on his feet," I ventured.

"Light on the feet" is a dancers' euphemism for gayer than laughter.

"Does he?" Lissa answered with a comfortable grin. She was settling in for a gossip fest, and shook off her running shoes. "Word is, David's a floater."

"Now," I continued, "is it possible that I didn't have a clue that Kendall double-dips from time to time? With David?"

"That's the scoop. Actually, it's no secret around here. But then, what is? As far as I know, Ken only slides with David. No one can figure it, though. David's a nice guy, but no DeNiro, you know? Of course, I haven't quite recovered from finding out about Malcolm Forbes."

I haven't even now. You've got to love a zillionaire who wears a kilt. I guess I was in the right place that day to indulge my men-in-skirts fetish. By the afternoon I'd be surrounded by hairy knees.

"So, that's why Frances was all bent out of shape," I said. "You know, I've known them for ten years now and I didn't have a clue." I had the feeling that Lissa was holding back, and hoped this might ease her into complete revelation.

"Neither did Frances until a couple of days ago. I suppose she didn't want to know. She thought the two of them were 'collaborating on a couple of projects.' That's the way it usually works."

I couldn't help but think of all those late-night conferences between Barry and Elaine over Kendall's financial management. I'm afraid my face flushed with mortification. Lissa didn't seem to notice; she was looking at our visitor.

"Bad news, Liss," said Jack Metelenis from the doorway. "Vic, right?" He held out his hand, and I shook it. "Can I bum

42

one of those?" He pointed to my cigarettes and I shook one out for him.

"I thought you quit," Lissa said, puffing away.

"I quit buying them." I lit it and handed it to him. "Unless I'm under unusual stress, which I am today. I sent one of the interns out to get me a pack. David Ogden called in sick, and Kendall is late, and I've got about forty thousand extras sitting around waiting for direction." He looked at me again. "By the way, we're almost ready to run you guys through your blocking."

I started to put out my cigarette, but Jack waved at me to stop. "You can't start without me," he said. "I tried calling Kendall, in case he overslept, but there's no answer. He's probably on his way. I don't want to go overtime today, though. The producers will have my head. Kendall's never late. Never. Do you have any idea where he is, Liss?"

"Not a glimmer."

"Damn. Well, if he gets here in the next twenty minutes, it won't matter, I guess." He stubbed out his cigarette. "All right, Vic, let's get this show on the road." I picked up my purse to follow. He turned and said, "Wardrobe didn't put you in that outfit, did they?"

I shook my head, trying not to take it personally. We walked past the extras' room. It was empty except for an array of deserted dance bags and reading material. The others had obviously been called to the set. I trailed slightly behind Jack into the elevator to go down the two floors to the studio.

"I could just wring Kendall's neck," he said. "Today, of all days. For years, I've been threatening to kill off his character. Finally, the writers give me what I want, and he doesn't show up."

"I thought he was the most popular guy on the show," I said.

"Are you kidding? He's the *only* popular character on the show. 'Raging Passions' has been going down the toilet for a couple of years now. I think Kendall's defection is going to be the final flush." The elevator doors opened and we stepped out.

"Then why would you want to kill off his character?"

"Oh, it was just a threat. Kendall is a compulsive perfectionist. He's always stopping production and arguing with me and the writers about his dialogue. He's a very expensive guy to have on the set." I saw the open doors to Studio B, where we were apparently going to be shooting. "But he was also the one who put the lox on the table, so to speak. Anyway, he's Steinbeck's problem now." An intern ran up and shoved a pack of cigarettes into Jack's hand without even slowing down. Metelenis lit up directly under the glow of a "No Smoking" sign, and started yelling, "Listen up, people . . ."

We extras were shuttled around like chess pieces and given stage direction for twenty minutes or so, and then sent to wardrobe. No one could accuse soap directors of over-rehearsing actors. I would have been nervous about my blocking if I'd really been given any.

My vital job, essentially, was to stand behind the bar. Well, not actually *stand*. Since I am an inch or two taller than Kendall, my job was to bend my knees slightly and *look* as if I were standing behind the bar.

Wardrobe inspected me with despair, and ended up handing me a white shirt and plaid skirt. Along with the fifteen or twenty other extras, I stripped off my clothes and tried my costume on. The shirt sleeves were too short, of course. So was the skirt, but since I was buried behind a bar, I didn't mention it. Finally, I was given a shirt off the men's rack and sent back to the Green Room.

Waiting rooms are always called "green rooms," though only one in ten is painted green. Probably because green is such an unflattering wall color. The extras' room was apple-green.

We waited throughout the morning without getting a call. I wished I'd eaten something for breakfast. My stomach was making noises like a steel-drum band. I didn't dare leave and get a Danish from the newsstand in the lobby for fear I'd miss

44

my big chance to be background stage dressing. From time to time, I sneaked off into Lissa's dressing room to smoke, but other than that, was well behaved.

By twelve-thirty, I was on the fine edge of both starvation and sensory deprivation. I'd read everything in my purse, including the instruction sheet from a travel case of tampons. At lunch, I planned to buy a book from a street vendor, just in case. To kill time, I lay down next to the tall guy on the floor and closed my eyes.

"Lunchtime," Brad announced.

I opened one eye and looked up at him standing over me. The room was empty again, except for the two of us. "You buying?" I asked.

"The network is," he said. "Everyone in the building knows that the 'Raging Passions' caterers are the best. "Too many vegetarians on 'Life Springs Eternal.' " He helped me to my feet. "Nice outfit. Could you change before anyone sees me with you?"

"Into what? A twenty-year-old?" The life of an extra is not all it could be, sometimes. I was hungry and, subsequently, being difficult again.

"You'll feel better after you eat. Come on."

We walked down the hall. We filled our plates from the buffet line, just behind the anchorman from the six-o'clock news. No one commented on why he and Brad were eating with actors. I complained between mouthfuls about having nothing to read. Brad handed me a paperback from his jacket pocket. It was *Essential Arabic, A Guidebook to Language and Culture,* compiled by Lexus, with Alex Chapman and Ashraf Ghali. Brad was covering the U.N. again, no doubt. I took it. I was that desperate.

"Listen up, people . . ." Jack Metelenis stood at the front of the dining room.

"Gotta go," said Brad, standing and clapping me on the back. "There's a Hasidic march in Brooklyn. The world needs to know." He sidled out a back door.

"Extras for the massacre-in-Scotland scenes can leave.

45

The good news is that you get to come back tomorrow. Leave costumes with wardrobe and have a good day."

Actors, being actors, lined up back at the buffet for seconds amid much good cheer over the prospect of an additional day of union work. Much as I wanted another ham-and-cheese sandwich, I chased after Jack.

"What's up?" I asked him.

"Do you have a cigarette?" he answered, not much to the point. I gave him one and he lit up under yet another "No Smoking" sign. "Thanks. Kendall still hasn't shown. I sent someone over to his apartment, but no answer. I have no idea where Frances is. Oh, Ken's probably just nursing a hangover, but I can't do any more shooting around him. And people wonder why I have an ulcer." Jack looked at the cigarette in his hand as though it were the first time he'd ever seen one, and said, "Anyway, you guys get another day."

"And lunch," I said. "I thought you bought a pack." I pointed at the cigarette hanging from his lip.

"I smoked them already," Jack shrugged. "I'm telling you, Kendall's trying to kill me." He started out the door. "By the way, great legs, ditch the skirt for tomorrow. Maybe I can sneak you an under-five."

"Longer or shorter?" I asked.

"Longer. Don't want you stealing focus."

I really hate that phrase.

Jack left, and I went back down the hall to give back my costume pieces and savor the possibility that I might get to speak on-camera the next day.

An "under-five" is simply that. It's a speaking role of under five lines. That's why you almost never see any of the faceless people on soap operas so much as grunt. One word, and the actor gets bumped up the pay scale.

Lissa caught me coming out of the extras' room. "Do you know where Kendall is? Did Jack say anything?"

I said, "No. I'm not exactly privy."

"Do you think Barry might know? Oh, it doesn't matter." But it was obvious she was concerned.

46

"Do you want me to call Barry and see?"

"Would you? I know it seems silly, but Kendall has never missed a day before. Hell, he's never even been late before. There's a phone in the production office. I'll show you." We followed a labyrinth of corridors and entered a suite of offices bathed in gray: walls, carpeting, chairs, everything. Lissa sat next to me as I dialed.

She said, "I was supposed to get blown up today in the terrorist bomb blast. Kendall, too. I just don't get it." She paused, waiting to see if I got a connection.

I was getting a creepy feeling. This, in itself, is nothing new to those who live in New York City, but I mean a *creepy* feeling. The same sort of sensation I got the time I was out of town doing *Annie* and Barry was having the affair with a paralegal. It was just there.

The phone rang four times and Barry's machine picked up. "Hi, this is Barry, and it's a beautiful spring day, so I'm out having a picnic. Leave a message at the beep, and I'll get back to you as soon as I can."

I thought that explained the creepy feeling. It was a Barry-creepy feeling. Not that he didn't have every right to have a picnic. Of course he did. I was still adjusting, though, and didn't want him having picnics willy-nilly with just any short accountant named Elaine that came along.

"Hi, Barry. This is me," I said, refusing as always to identify myself by name to his machine. After ten years, he ought to know my voice. "Lissa and I were wondering if you've heard anything from Kendall. We're here on the set and he isn't. I'm headed home, so give me a call there when you get the fried chicken out of your teeth." Why did I have to say that? Damn, damn, damn. Maybe he'd think I was just kidding. Of course he wouldn't. He'd know I was jealous. Damn, damn, damn. I shrugged to Lissa. "Guess we'll have to wait until tomorrow to find out."

I was wrong.

CHAPTER
FIVE

B *lahhhhhhhhhhht.*

My intercom buzzer blasted while I was in the closet. Surprised, I stood up too quickly from where I was rooting around the dozens of pairs of shoes piled on the floor. My hair got caught in a hanger dangling from the hem of my black audition dress. The buzzer squawked again and longer. I ripped the wire hanger out of my coif (such as it was, after an hour in a very small closet) and dashed to the intercom before it could go off again. *Blahhhhhhhhhht.* Too late.

In a successful attempt to raise everyone's rent, my landlord had installed an intercom system that sounded like a crazed Nazi ripping through the base of the skull with a dull chain saw. I believe it cost about a buck forty-five.

I opened my peephole and looked down the outer corridor and out the grated slot in the exterior building door. That selfsame landlord had considerately trashed the carved oak doors with the etched glass to install the "women-in-chains" brown metal job with heavy-gauge chicken wire to create a six-inch-square opening. The city approved this as a major capital improvement, and raised my rent six dollars a month—in perpetuity—to pay for it.

Aesthetic violation doesn't come cheap in Manhattan.

Dan, the cop with the moral code, waved at me and pushed open the door. Did I mention this new door doesn't always lock? I opened my apartment door. Dan limped toward me.

"What's wrong with your leg?" I asked, wondering at the same time if I had gotten so old and crumpled that I could only garner interest from guys with bad joints. It was not a pleasant train of thought.

"Just let me sit down," he said, squeezing his considerable bulk past me, and swooping Slasher up in one huge hand. He kissed the cat on the nose and dropped him before unstrapping his shoulder holster and shoving it and his service revolver into my canned-goods cabinet. Gimping his way back to the living room, he picked up Slasher again and sprawled on the couch. "Is that a good boy?" he babbled at the cat. "*What* a good boy!" Slasher craned up and gently bit Dan's nose. No, I have no idea why the cat does that. But he has never drawn blood. "Would you turn on the news, babe?"

Only two people in the world have ever called me "babe." One was a bookie, the other a cop. Go figure. I flicked on the television.

"Do we have a date?" I asked, a bit ragged.

"Yes, but I'm two hours early. Do you have a beer, by any chance? It's real hot out there"—he shifted, rolling up his shirt sleeves—"and I've been running." The hair on his arms was wet, sure enough.

"How could you be running on that leg?" I persisted, as I got a Coors out of the fridge. "And why are you two hours early for a date I didn't think we had?"

"I didn't have the bum leg when I was running." He took the beer and I went for a coaster in hopes of salvaging the finish on my Victorian coffee table. "I was chasing down a bad guy." He took a long swig of the beer. "Could you turn the volume up a little? I think I'm on-camera, taking the perp into the station."

Sure enough, there Dan was, bustling a man about half his size through a crowd of reporters. I was confused. Dan is a desk cop/investigator, and he wasn't limping on the tape.

"You aren't limping there," I said inanely.

"Nahh. I screwed up my leg on the way over here with some other yutz. Criminals are so annoying," he contended, taking another sip. "They're so *silly.* I'm walking down the street, minding my own business, and this idiot rips off this woman's neck chain about a foot away from me. I mean, I am in this guy's *face."* Dan spread his arms wide for inspection. "Now do, or do I *not* look like the fuzz?" No response necessary there. He couldn't look more like the fuzz if he had it printed on his forehead. Dan plunged on further into the diatribe, "All I had to do was reach over and nail him." I nodded my attentiveness. "So I do, and this cretin looks at me, and I know he's *finally* got me pegged as the man, the bozo. So what does this genius do? He runs. He weighs about forty-four pounds and he *runs.* It's so *silly.* Can I have another one of these?" He held up the empty can. I went to get another and he continued. "So I catch up with this creepo in about fifteen feet, and he decides to *struggle."* The insanity of this decision seemed to overwhelm Dan. He shook his head in disbelief. "I mean, I outweigh him by about eighty pounds. Anyway, I'm forced to throw him to the ground and put my knee in his back until backup arrives. As the white shields are taking him away, he turns and cracks me one in the foot." He took off his shoes and wiggled his toes. "Nothing broken, but, jeez, it hurts. All I want is a hot shower, and I end up chasing down a bad guy with the IQ of a paramecium."

Dan is obviously not stupid. It aggravates him inordinately to spend time arresting people who are.

"So, we *do* have a date," I observed during the lull.

"Yeah. Remember? I said if the bust went down early enough, we should have dinner. Of course I didn't know I was going to be sitting on a goofball on my way over. Okay if I just

50

order in Chinese?" he said, phone already in his hand. I nodded and he hit the autodial. Yes, the Chinese restaurant around the corner is entered in my autodial. I'm an actor.

Dan patted what little remained available on my sofa, and I sat next to him while he ordered, figuring to catch the weather on TV so I'd know how recalcitrant my hair was going to be for the next day on "RP." A picture of Kendall James filled the little block over one shoulder of the anchorman. I bounced up and turned up the sound. Dan started, "I got the Pu Pu Pl—" I shushed him.

The anchorman sonorously pronounced, "This just in. Kendall James, star of 'Raging Passions,' and slated to star in the much-touted new series 'SPA!' has been found dead in his luxury East Side apartment. Production staff on the daytime drama became concerned when James did not report to the set for shooting early this morning. James's wife, Frances, has not been located, and police are deeming the actor's death 'suspicious.' More on this story as further information becomes available. Next up, a new baby walrus in the Bronx—" I turned the sound back down.

"Oh, my God," I said and plunked myself down next to Dan.

"Life in the city," Dan muttered world-wearily. "I hope you like spicy."

"What?"

"I got the General Tso's chicken, extra hot. How's your ulcer these days?"

"I was at a party with him, just last night."

"General Tso?"

"Kendall." I tried to figure out if Dan was joking and couldn't tell.

"Bummer." He kissed me. "Could you turn up the sound a little? I want to catch the sports." I glared at him. He looked a bit startled. "Did you know him well, or something?" Slasher had crawled up under Dan's jersey and was trying to bite a cop-hand through the fabric. The cat's back feet were

51

pumping, reminding me of the parasitic birth scene from *Alien.*

"Yes. Well, not *well,* but for around ten years, casually. I'm doing day work on 'RP' this week, thanks to Kendall. I can't believe it." The phone rang. I reached across Dan's pulsating belly to answer it. "Hello?"

"Don't you ever pick up your messages?" It was Barry. "I left three messages on your machine; where have you been?"

"In the closet. Have you heard about Kendall?"

"Why do you think I've been trying to get ahold of you? Jack Metelenis had the super open Kendall's apartment, and they found the body. Jack called me. Do you know where Frances is?"

"How would I know that?" I asked. Just because I'm nosy, Barry thinks I know where everyone is at all times.

"Sometimes you just know these things," he answered, fairly enough. Sometimes I just do. "The police need to talk to her. I'm afraid she may have been kidnapped. What do you think?"

I concentrated for a moment and got no bad vibes. "I think she's fine." That felt right, anyway. "How did he die? What did they mean by 'suspicious'?"

"They're performing an autopsy, of course. We should know how he died sometime tomorrow. I'm afraid some people think Frances might have done it. I represent her, too, and I'd better talk to her as soon as I can. Her disappearance doesn't look good."

"No." The door buzzer exploded. I carried the phone to the peephole, saw the Chinese deliveryman, and buzzed him in. Juggling the phone, I held out my hand to Dan for money and opened my door. The courier held up the bag so I could inspect the bill. I handed him the twenty-dollar bill and waved him away. "I'll call you if I hear anything."

"Call if you even *feel* anything. I hate trials. Maybe we can get this cleared up before I have to make a court appearance," Barry said.

"We?"

"Just because we're having marital difficulties doesn't mean I don't depend on you."

Right. "I thought you were depending on Elaine," I said, drawing out her name like a wad of gum.

"Don't say her name through your nose like that. Elaine happens to be extremely distraught over Kendall's death. She had to go to her country home to pull herself together."

Personally, I have never considered Montauk, Long Island, to be the "country."

"Why didn't you go with her?" I asked bitchily.

"She needs some time alone. Besides, there are records the police are going to need. One of us has to be here." Barry cleared his throat and changed the subject. "Anyway, Frances calls you when she's in trouble. You know how unstable she is. Maybe she'll call you now for crystal-ball gazing or something."

"You know I don't do that."

"Frances thinks you do. So, call, okay? Maybe your friend Brad knows something. Will you get back to me?"

"Yes, if I hear anything." I hung up, a little surprised at Barry's outpouring of concern for the new widow.

Dan had gotten out the chopsticks and plates and was laying waste to the delivered food. I went to the kitchen and got us both a beer.

"Dan?" I began.

"No," he answered before he heard the question. "Have a fried dumpling."

"Dan," I resumed stubbornly.

"No." He outstubborned me. "The cold sesame noodles are great. Here, have some." He piled some on my plate and fed one by hand to Slasher, who is extremely fond of Szechuan food.

"If you could just make one phone call, that's all. A friend of mine has died under mysterious circumstances," I cajoled.

53

"A 'casual' friend," Dan amended. "Sounds to me like it's your husband who's most interested."

"Ex-husband."

"Not quite, but that's another story, isn't it? Forget it. Getting you information on a case that is under investigation is a clear violation of the public trust. Go on, eat." He popped a dumpling into his mouth, whole.

Just my luck to be going out with a bona-fide, dyed-in-the-wool ethical cop with a jealous streak. Obviously, I have very bad karma. I wheedled, sulked, begged, and reasoned throughout the entire meal—to no avail.

Lucky for me, our intrepid reporter, Brad, had fewer scruples—something about the public's right to know—but he wouldn't be home from location until nine or ten o'clock.

Dan fed Slasher enough sesame noodles to fill a doberman, as I pleaded my case. When Slasher threw up on the carpet, Dan rose and hobbled to the kitchen cabinet to retrieve his gun. He tore off a couple of paper towels on his way back to the living room, strapped on his .38, and bent over to clean up the rug. He grunted heavily as he pulled himself upright.

"It is obvious to me that you're going to be impossible until you get what you want. Since I'm not going to give it to you, I've going to go home and soak my foot in peace and quiet." He kissed me very gently and pressed the squishy paper toweling into my hand. "I'll call you tomorrow to let you know if I've recovered from my in-the-line-of-duty injury. Maybe we can go to a movie," he said before he tweaked Slasher's nose and left.

As I wrapped the leftovers, I thought about Kendall. How brutally ironic that, just on the brink of making the big, big time, he was dead. And how? According to the news report, the authorities had some evidence to suspect foul play. But why? Kendall was, after all, just an actor.

When figures like Ghandi, Kennedy, or Martin Luther King get bumped off, you know there is some misguided geopolitical motivation at play somewhere. Actors are a more benign lot, over all. In fact, actors spend much of their lives being other people, rather than themselves. Every so often a psychotic fan gets carried away with murderous intent—John Lennon was killed not more than eight blocks from where I live—but that notion just didn't feel right to me. Statistically, most homicides are committed by those known to the victim.

That could very well finger the late Kendall's missing wife—widow—Frances.

I turned off the lights in the living room, put the leftovers in the refrigerator, and went back into the bedroom. It looked as if a bomb had hit it.

Clothes and shoes were strewn over every inch of the floor and bed. I plucked the ruffled white blouse from the top of the heap that I'd chosen to wear to the set the next day, but couldn't find the skirt I'd picked out. It took nearly an hour to get things back on hangers and into the closet. Most of the tops I pseudo-folded and rammed into drawers. Typically, I had left the skirt I was trying to relocate in the bathroom so I wouldn't lose it in the disorder. Disgusted with myself, I hung the miraculously restored skirt with the blouse, turned on the bedroom television, and tucked myself into bed. Brad was on the screen doing a commentary on racial harmony. He was in favor of it. It reminded me to give him a call.

I pushed Slasher off the telephone, where he'd decided to spend the night, and dialed. When a woman answered, I hung up, turned off the TV, set the alarm, and tried to sleep.

The woman on the other end of the line could have been Brad's daughter, visiting from Oregon. But, of course, I knew she wasn't.

I should have been glad that Brad's old skiing accident hadn't totally debilitated him, but, of course, I wasn't.

That creepy feeling was washing over me again, and I didn't think it had to do with Brad's extracurricular activities. To paraquote a song from the murder-musical *Something's Afoot:* something *was* afoot, and . . . the butler didn't do it.

CHAPTER SIX

Wardrobe approved my new costume, and by bringing my own outfit, I would get paid a few extra bucks, too. I hurried back down to the dressing-room area. I could hear Lissa sobbing from the moment the elevator doors opened. It didn't take any particular sensitivity to figure out that she'd heard the news about the late Kendall James.

Hiccuping sounds told me she had nearly stopped her crying, but when she saw me, Lissa resumed with a vengeance.

Barry has always claimed that I have that effect on people.

"Oh, Vic, it was murder," she moaned.

I went over to where Lissa was sitting at her dressing table, and knelt down beside her. She threw her arms around me. "And they think I may have done it!" she wailed. "The autopsy showed that Kendall was poisoned. The police were at my apartment first thing this morning. They think I may have done it."

"Who could think something like that?" I soothed, but that nasty feeling was crawling around my insides again.

"Who? I don't remember their names," she snuffled. "There was a big guy, real scary. He looked like he hated me. It was awful!"

I smoothed her hair and noticed she was a real blonde. What kind of a cop could hate a natural blonde?

"Duchinski?" I asked, already knowing the answer.

"What?"

"Could it have been a Sergeant Dan Duchinski?"

"That's right! Did he see you, too?" She blew her nose vigorously.

I frowned. "Not this morning." That rat. The whole time he was pretending to ignore me, he was getting curious. I didn't have a doubt in the world that the big rodent had actually requested to be assigned to the case. "I'm sure no one really suspects you," I lied smoothly. "Where did they think Kendall was given the poison?"

"They don't know for sure. The sergeant thought it must have happened at Barry's party. I just can't stand it."

Before I could utter another false reassurance, a techie appeared at the door and told Lissa she was needed on the set. She carefully patted the tears from under her eyes and blew her nose, again. After a deep breath, and not a word, she walked numbly out of the room. I lit a cigarette, took a drag, and stubbed it out.

If there was a suspicion that the poison had been administered at the party, I reasoned, Dan would be grilling poor Barry just about now. The hateful part of me didn't mind all that much, even though I couldn't imagine Barry as homicidal. Me, perhaps, but not him. Barry has never struck me as the physically injurious type, and certainly not someone who would deliberately part with a percentage.

I yelled into the extras' room, "If anyone needs me, tell them I'm in number four, on twelve," and headed off to see Brad the rat-stud. Clearly, this was not going to be a good-attitude-toward-the-male-of-the-species day.

I guess there were no international incidents that morning

because Brad was in his cubicle, dozing. Must have been a long night on the domestic front.

I wanted to kick the chair out from under him. Yes, I realize how hypocritical I was being. I realized it then, too. It didn't help. I slapped one of his feet propped on the desk. Rather hard, I believe, because he jolted awake and nearly propelled himself to the carpet.

"Rise and shine, Merry Sunshine," I said, not very originally. "I need your brain."

"Huh?" he muttered cleverly.

I put his mug with the network logo, filled with oil-slicked cold coffee, in his hand and steered it to his mouth. Journalists, like actors, can ingest caffeine in any state. "Wake up. I don't have much time," I said, sitting on the corner of his desk and watching him take a couple of swigs. "Are you covering the James murder?"

"Huh?" he gurgled through a mouthful of liquid. "Who?"

"Kendall James," I said patiently. "From the party two nights ago? The actor?" I thought Brad was coming around to the land of the living, but on the off-chance I'd misjudged, threw him more specific identification. "The dead one?"

"Oh, yeah. Kendall." He was showing signs of consciousness. "What was the question?"

"Are you, by some stroke of luck, covering the story?"

"Shit, no," he said, aggrieved, "that's a fluff piece." Brad stood up and stretched expansively.

When did murder become "fluffy"?

"Look," I persisted, "I'm on a time schedule here. Who *is* tracking this thing?"

"Beverly!" Brad yelled over the partition, "Who was assigned the eighty-sixed-actor piece?"

Apparently, there is little dignity in death around the average American newsroom.

A faceless female voice responded, "Frannie."

"Kaulfuss got stuck with it." He said to me, and sat back down. "Why?"

58

"There's some stuff I'd like to know." Which I thought was perfectly obvious.

"Why?" he asked, as though it mattered.

At my age, I now refuse to believe I'm stupid. I also *usually* refuse to acknowledge any intimation of this belief from others. Oh, well, what's one more resolution down the toilet of life? "Because I knew him, and several other people I know—or was married to—appear to be suspects." I took a cigarette out of his pack and lit it, finishing with the only argument that would truly sway him, "And because I'm nosy and will not let you rest until you tell me absolutely everything you know, suspect, or can beg, borrow, or steal from other sources."

Brad took the cigarette from my fingers, took a long drag, and wearily yelled over the partition again, "Beverly!"

Out of nowhere came the anonymous Beverly's dulcet yell. "She's on location trying to get something from the lawyer. Her notes are in the main computer. Access 'James comma K,' and leave me alone. I have work to do."

So much for privacy and professional respect.

Brad swung his chair to the left, slipped his glasses over his nose, and, one finger at a time, pecked in the access code. Almost immediately, the display screen filled with text, and Brad's phone rang.

"Sinclair," he identified himself into the mouthpiece. His eyes scanned the screen. "Yeah," was all he said, hung up, and continued reading. A smile flickered across his face. "Looks like your ex is a prime suspect."

"What?" I leaned over his shoulder to read Kaulfuss's notes. There were a lot of typos, but, sure enough, Barry had been called to police headquarters that morning for interrogation.

Brad read along with me, and said, "Don't worry about that. The cops probably just wanted to see Kendall's financial records. It's standard operating procedure in these cases." Brad bit me on the neck. "Oh, and you're wanted on the set."

"What?"

59

I know, I was being repetitive. I tried speed-reading the screen, but the thought of losing a paycheck was interfering with my usual comprehension.

"Can you give me a printout, or is that a violation of something?" I badgered.

Actors, who mostly do what they do out of some bizarre "creative" place, don't understand much about rules of ethical behavior in business, but we're mostly smart enough to know that the rules exist.

"Sure *is* a violation," Brad said, and hit the print command. The printer started spitting out paper within seconds. "Everyone will hear this crap tonight, anyway."

Actually, as we all know, only Edna Sandberg and the two Chinese ladies on my third floor were likely to hear this particular account, but it was more than I'd hoped for. I ripped the pages from the printer, kissed Brad before I remembered I was annoyed with him for not being obsessed with me, and said, "Thanks." He waved me off, completely not obsessed.

As I steered myself to the corner for the exit to get back to my "job," Beverly's disembodied voice trilled over the din of telephones and computers, "The stuff marked with an asterisk is off the record, Vic. Don't make any public statements or we'll have to throw you to the wolves."

"Gotcha, Bev," I shouted into the air halfway to the elevator, already reading the printout. I was interrupted by the opening of doors, pressing of buttons, closing of doors, checking of watch, and all those things that one does in and around elevators. I'd only gotten through Kendall's background bio when the elevator doors opened. I stepped out, nose in paper, and heard Lissa.

"Vic," she said, running toward me, "we're supposed to be on the set. Hold the elevator."

I was getting very good at holding elevators. My finger went immediately to "door open." At the same moment, I saw plainly written on the second computer sheet something even old, jaded me found hard to believe.

When Lissa was in the car, I punched the floor of the sound stage, and looked closely at her profile for confirmation of my hunch. Yes, what I had read in the notes was true. It didn't make any sense, but it was definitely fact.

"Were you really engaged to marry David Ogden?" I blurted out as the elevator doors opened. Lissa herself had told me that David was as gay as donned apparel. She looked at me curiously, as one looks at a foreigner with an indecipherable accent.

Jack Metelenis's director's voice resounded down the hall, "Listen up, people . . ."

"We'd better hurry," Lissa said and dashed toward the open doors to the set. I ran after her. Lissa is very fast for a woman with normal-length legs.

It probably has something to do with youth.

I squeezed into the door, on tiptoe to see over the heads of the other latecomers. I could see that Lissa had made it through the crowd and was standing next to David Ogden a few feet from Jack on the massacre-in-Scotland pub set.

"As you all know, this is Dana Fisher," Jack said, indicating the woman in her late fifties at his side.

Dana Fisher was (and is) a soap-opera legend. She had been the creator of at least seven major soaps over the previous three decades, executive producer of five. Her gray hair was cut very short, and very chic, exposing huge, dangling coin earrings. The cut of her expansively draped teal silk wrap denoted all the glamour of her daytime fantasies, and screamed money, money, money.

"I'm sure you're all aware of the tragedy that occurred last night," Jack continued. "Of course, we will all miss Kendall James very much, and are devastated over the loss of such a fine man and actor." Dana Fisher nodded solemnly in confirmation. Jack went on, "*But* the show must go on." So much for sentimentality. "Dana and I are going to be huddling with the writers to come up with a story line that will work for 'RP,' in light of Kendall's passing. 'Raging Passions' is far too important to the viewing public to let them down, so we are going to do our damnedest for them." Another serious nod from Dana. "Kendall would have wanted it that way."

I wasn't at all sure that Kendall would have given a damn, but Jack was doing one hell of a job bolstering the troops.

"So," Jack said, "I want all of you to take the morning to compose yourselves, and report back after lunch—say, two-ish. We should have some pages for you by then." Dana whispered something to Jack, but all he said was, "That's all. See you at two."

Jack and Dana walked to the exit at the rear of the room as the crew and cast started piling past me, through the double doors to the hallway. I did my best to stay out of the line of traffic by hugging the interior wall with my backside. When the crowd had thinned sufficiently, I wove my way to the video cameras, where Lissa and David were talking in frustratingly low voices.

That overwhelming feeling—that I knew something— was nagging at me. I fervently wished that *what* I felt I knew would come, too. Sometimes the feeling needs a push. Like with some brazen snooping.

Trying to appear innocent, I presented myself behind Lissa and put my hand on her forearm. "Are you all right?" I asked her, and looked quizzically at David Ogden, waiting for a formal introduction. Lissa spun around.

"Oh," she said. "Yes, I'm fine, Vic." She saw my look, and did her duty. "Vic, this is David. David, this is Vic Bowering, she's married to Barry Laskin, Kendall's attorney."

"Temporarily," I said, offering my hand. I knew I was in the right place the second David shook it. The sensation was that of a dull electrical pulse looking for a conductor. That's me: an irregularly efficient psychic lightning rod. "Are you feeling better?" I asked him, hoping to hone in on a lie, or the truth. Whatever. "We missed you on the set yesterday."

Lissa answered for him, "A twenty-four-hour bug."

"Yeah," David contributed. "I'm fine now."

62

But he didn't look it. Handsome, yes, but vaguely dissipated. He was hiding something, and so was Lissa.

"David has a reading for Steinbeck for 'SPA!' this afternoon, don't you, David?" Lissa said. I wondered why she was being so damned helpful. I doubted David needed much mothering.

"Right!" David confirmed, with the obligatory exclamation point. "I'd better get at those 'SPA!' pages, too. Excuse me. Don't want to look unprepared for my shot at the big time!"

I had no doubt that David's sentiment was genuine there. He kissed Lissa quickly on the lips, ignored me, and scuttled away. I didn't think I'd be adding David Ogden to my Christmas-card list.

"He really is very sweet," Lissa said defensively, watching his exit.

I politely, and, I hope, convincingly, said, "I'm sure." When I noticed the computer sheets still dangling from my right hand, I remembered my initial unanswered question. "You must have cared about him to have been engaged to marry him."

Lissa looked relieved. "Oh, that," she smiled. "The engagement was just a publicity stunt dreamed up by Dana Fisher, the producer. Dumb, huh? We were dying in the ratings, and she thought that, since the television romance between David and me wasn't working, maybe a real one would." She grinned again, appreciating my naïveté, and my embarrassment over having it. "Dana's a grasping, avaricious bitch—but a smart one. The ratings staggered up a bit. Not enough to make much of a difference to our sponsors." Lissa laughed, and twirled a length of her blond hair into a tight coil around her finger. "The public was so bored, they didn't even notice when the real marriage didn't happen." We both raised our eyes skyward at the whole concept of publicity engagements. Lissa's eyes flashed with an idea. "Want to have brunch? We can sit in the smoking section!"

My stomach was ranting emptily at me, so I said, "You're

63

on," the news reporter's notes momentarily forgotten in my hand, in light of the prospect of restaurant food. Yet we didn't make it within fifteen feet of escape. Dana Fisher and Jack reentered from the rear door.

"Lissa!" Jack shouted, coming toward us, Dana by his side, and both looking grim. I was getting that "invisible" feeling again. "Hi, Vic," he tossed in my general direction, not bothering to introduce me to Dana. Instinctively knowing I was nobody, the producer didn't ask either. "Lissa, we have to talk."

Dana interrupted Jack with, "You're going to have to pick up a lot of slack here in the story line, Liss. We're counting on you." Dana put her arm around Lissa's shoulder and started walking her to the bar stools on the set.

I had discovered an advantage to invisibility. Since no one seemed able to see me, I tagged along. The three of them sat. I floated around the perimeter as innocuously as I could manage.

"I know you planned to die today," Dana intoned, obviously ignorant of the irony in the statement, "but we think it would be better for the show now if you recovered and mourned for an extended period of time. Audiences are very partial to deep suffering, as you know."

I knew that. Overdue weddings and profound grief really make people tune in.

"Now," Dana continued, "it's possible you've lined up some work, but you have a contract with us through the end of the year, and we're going to have to hold you to it."

This, for those of you who read a lot of entertainment gossip, will be familiar to you as the same heartbreaking scenario that cost Pierce Brosnan the role of James Bond, when "Remington Steele" was unexpectedly picked up for another season. Hi-ho, the glamorous life.

Lissa's face remained impassive, hard as a pretty piece of rose quartz. I could almost hear her heart beating in the short silence that followed, but she said nothing.

64

Jack interjected, "Of course, we can probably find an extra buck or two for your inconvenience."

Dana glared at him, so briefly, if I had not been watching her so closely, I wouldn't have noticed. She nodded pleasantly. More silence.

"Well," Lissa said after another pulsating pause, "I don't see that I have any choice, do I?" Dana tried to look sorry, and shrugged. The producer was no actor, that was for sure. "When do I get my pages?" Lissa asked with resignation.

But Lissa wasn't resigned. I was certain.

"We're going to talk about that during the break," said Dana, "because, even though you have to live, Ogden's getting the ax."

"Dana!" Jack blurted, very uncomfortably.

"This is not open for discussion, Metelenis," Dana said through her teeth. "I have had it up the ass with Ogden's pills, grass, and absenteeism. Now that Kendall is history, the boy-toy goes. I hope I don't have to remind you who's in charge here."

Jack leaned back on his heels and lowered his chin, all the while holding Dana's gaze. He was annoyed, but not particularly angry, that I could see. No doubt the director had been bludgeoned with this power play hundreds of times before over the years. I could, however, feel almost palpable waves of hostility pounding from the demonstrably self-contained Lissa. I admired her restraint, especially taking into account her relatively young age. I knew that the larger members of the tech crew would have had to peel me off the ceiling—or the producer's face—under similar circumstances.

Dana said, "We're having food sent in. We need the principals in the writers' conference room ASAP, Liss." She turned away, considering the matter closed.

"Vic and I were going to go out for a bite," Lissa countered, objecting, I guessed, out of spite.

Dana glanced over her shoulder at me, reaffirming my nobodyness.

"Tough," the producer said, and bustled out the rear door.

"Sorry," Jack grumbled to both Lissa and me as he followed Dana into the bowels of the sound-stage floor.

"Sorry," Lissa reiterated, "the bitch queen decrees."

"It's okay. Business first." I couldn't really afford restaurant food, anyway. "I'm sorry whatever projects you had lined up have to be shit-canned."

That's actor-talk. Sorry, Mom.

"Oh, I didn't have anything lined up." Lissa grinned widely. "As a matter of fact, I was scared to death I wouldn't be able to get anything this good again. Things couldn't be better."

My respect for Lissa as an actor had just risen geometrically. She waved at me as she trailed after Dana and poor, beleaguered Jack.

I left the building with more than just my stomach gnawing at me. Realizing I was still clutching the best that TV journalism had to offer in my hand, I called Jewel from the next corner and asked her to expect me.

Since I'd gotten a message on my answering machine telling me not to bother to return to the 'RP' set that day, Jewel and I went ahead and got pleasantly blitzed on a special bottle of Cristal Brut that her bridge partners had left the night before.

Cristal is my favorite champagne. As it costs something around a kazillion dollars a bottle, I wish I'd never been exposed to its considerable charms. Fortunately or unfortunately, depending upon how one views life, it was an accidental discovery that happened over a staggeringly expensive candlelight dinner with Sergio—the only count I've ever met who actually has money—a few months prior. These little acquired tastes are the reason I've never eaten caviar or snorted cocaine. In my precarious financial position, who needs another prohibitively costly preference?

"So, you're off tomorrow, too?" Jewel asked between

sips. She was ensconced in her customary place on the couch, feet up, perusing the bootleg notes I had gotten from Brad.

"Yes. A memorial service for Kendall." I placed the Brie and crackers on the coffee table next to her. "It was a nice gesture to allow everyone to go," I said, and plunked myself down on the Oriental carpet where I could reach the cheese and the wine.

"Bullshit," said Jewel benignly. "Obviously, the writing staff is behind in the rewrites." She delicately sliced the Brie and placed it on a water cracker. "Have some of the Jordan almonds in the dish behind you. Wonderful with a dry champagne." I grabbed a handful and munched thoughtfully, watching her read.

When she had stacked the papers neatly and topped her glass, I asked, "Well?"

"Well," Jewel answered, "I think your husband is in the deep shit."

"Barry? Whatever for?"

Jewel thrust a page of Kaulfuss's research into my hand. "This telephone interview with the accountant."

"Elaine," I said, my eyes scanning the page. "Why didn't I see this?"

"The pages were stuck together." Jewel munched some trail mix and watched me calmly.

"But this says that Elaine has been concerned about discrepancies in Kendall's books for a few months. Why would she say that? Barry's her"—my tongue caught on the word, but I managed finally to say it—"lover. Why would she implicate him that way?"

"Perhaps because it's true. It says, right there, that Elaine was reluctant." When I made no comment, Jewel went on, "I should think so. I doubt she's the kind of woman who'd marry someone practicing law from behind bars."

"Oh, my God."

"Exactly. You said yourself that Barry is spending money like a drunken Ph.D." She ticked items off on her fingers. "The co-op; big parties; stupid electrical kitchenware; a girlfriend with high expectations."

"What do you think, Jewel?"

"I think that if Barry gets sent up the river, you can steal back your appliances," she pronounced. "But you seem to think he's innocent, and I trust your instincts more than you do, so we can temporarily forget that side benefit." She poured the dregs of the bottle into my glass.

"But will the police agree with me?"

"Doubtful." Jewel put her hand to her chin and continued, "But on the bright side, if I have this right, the cops are investigating a slew of suspects here. This tells me there was more to our Kendall James than we thought. By the way, though it would have been great publicity, I note you're not anywhere on this list.

"For our purposes—i.e., bagging the guilty party—we should concentrate on the people attending Barry's party, since logically that is where the poison was administered." Jewel must have seen the panic in my eyes, because she was quick to add, "And for simplicity's sake, we should move those who would stand to profit from Kendall's continued good health to the bottom of the list. That would be"—she squinted a bit and picked up a pencil—"Barry"—she put a check next to his name—"because a dead client doesn't generate much income from which an agent can derive a percentage—and, if he really had stolen that money and weren't a proven cheap son of a bitch, you'd be getting alimony."

"I didn't ask for alimony," I defended Barry, knowing Jewel had only checked him off out of deference for me.

"And next time, you'll know to talk with me." Jewel sipped thoughtfully. "Hmmm. David Ogden"—she passed over his name—"had no stake in Kendall's demise because he's a perfectly dreadful performer and couldn't act his way out of a parking ticket stark-naked. His job, as you said, ended about the minute that Kendall's did."

"But," I argued, desperate for another suspect, "since Kendall's murder, the producer is extending contracts. Lissa, for example, was supposed to get knocked off, but now will be staying on because of rewrites."

"But not Ogden," Jewel retaliated. "And besides, no one could have predicted that."

"But," I bounced back, "Ogden was Kendall's lover. Maybe he was jealous. It could have been a quarrel."

"Poison," Jewel noted soberly, "is not a crime-of-immediate-passion murder weapon. Had Kendall been beaten to death, or shot, you might have a point. Anyway, wouldn't Ogden have been let go eventually no matter what?"

"Maybe," I conceded, "except firing him could have prevented any guest appearance on 'RP' by Kendall in the future, if Ken got loyal. So David would want him alive, just in case." I got up and went to the kitchen for another bottle of bubbly, albeit not Cristal. I was too loaded to be fussy or know when to stop. Jewel was, as always, stone-cold sober. I plunked back down on the carpet and finished the thought. "I'm telling you, Jewel, even though you think he's innocent of murder, there's something rotten about Ogden, and it isn't just his acting. He has a drug problem, and something else I can't quite put my finger on."

"Okay." She erased the check next to Ogden's name, and replaced it with a question mark. "Now, what about the ingenue, Lissa Stevens? Did she want out of her contract?"

"No. As a matter of fact, she's kind of thrilled to be staying on."

"Excellent. Finally, a real suspect. Only two things would have saved Lissa's job: Kendall staying, or Kendall dying. Poison's a woman's weapon, you know."

I remembered reading that somewhere. Or maybe I'd just heard it on "Jeopardy!" But Lissa? Things were getting fuzzy.

"Now," Jewel went on, "the wife has disappeared. Very suspicious. But, despite her husband's dalliance, he didn't seem to have plans to dump her. And if she wanted to kill him, wouldn't it have been better to wait until after he'd piled up the big bucks on the new series? Sit up, darling, and pay attention." I'd lain down for a rest, but roused myself. "Of course, she may simply be dead, too, her body disposed of in some clever way. You've done her tarot; what do you think?"

I sat back up and said, "No. She's alive." It was just a feeling, but my feelings are most reliable when I'm menstruating, or drunk, or during the full of the moon. Don't ask me why, I don't make the rules. Illogically, I perked up and said, "She does have a hysterical streak." Then, feeling remorseful for assassinating the emotional character of a possibly dead person, I added, "But then, don't we all?"

"Aha!" Jewel beamed. "Then there you have it. By the process of elimination. Runaway wife equals murderess." She leaned over the coffee table and inspected me closely. "Now I think you'd better run along and take a nap."

I don't know that I said anything in response to this excellent advice. I do know I ended up forgetting my shoes. Thank heavens for the gods of fools and actors that I live in the building next to Jewel's.

"And would you mail those letters for me on the way to the memorial service tomorrow?" Jewel said as I reached the door. I took them and staggered down the stairs and, ultimately, into my own apartment.

As I drifted off into a foggy slumber, pretzeled on my very short sofa, with Slasher snoring happily where he was sprawled on his back across my bent knees, I remember thinking that Jewel and I weren't even close to the truth.

Or maybe I was ignoring it.

CHAPTER
SEVEN

Were it possible to die from a hangover, a lot of people would have been saved a great deal of trouble at my hands. But it is not, and they weren't.

I awoke on the sofa the morning of Kendall's memorial service, limbs cramped into a Quasimodo configuration, with Slasher breathing tuna breath directly into my nostrils. He is a fabulous animal who neither yowls nor slaps at my face in the morning to let me know he needs nutrition. However, I leave it to your imagination to conjure up the sensory image of cat breath up the nose first thing upon awakening with a champagne hangover.

My legs refused to straighten any more than the limbs of Lucy, the unearthed Australopithicus, so it was with a loping struggle that I made it to the bathroom. To my surprise, once there, I didn't barf.

Nonetheless, I couldn't bring myself to look in the mirror, either. Bath, toothbrushing (three times), and other rituals accomplished, I fed Slasher and checked the clock. Befuddled as I was, I'd slept through the entire morning. The memorial service was in half an hour.

Fortunately, I have a black rayon dress, especially purchased for funerals, so I didn't have to tax my brain with fashion decisions. I put on my makeup in bed, with the lights off and the shutters closed.

Riverview Chapel, where the memorial service was to be held, was all of three blocks away from my apartment. The day was oppressively hot for the month of May, and the sun excruciatingly bright for a hung-over human. The air had that singularly New York taste of old Chinese food and aluminum pots. As I approached Riverview, I spotted the throng of people spilling into the avenue.

A few years before, I would have looked for the police cars or fire trucks to validate the presence of such a mob, but after fifteen years in New York, I knew that heinous crime scenes and fires don't draw all that much attention. There were blue police barricades set up around the block surrounding the pseudo-Gothic chapel entrance. Jack Metelenis was positioned at the only opening, along with a squad of security guards. When he spotted me, he spoke to one of the uniformed men and I was allowed through.

"What the hell's going on?" I sputtered, perspiration drizzling down my forehead. A drop slid down the side of my nose, like a tear.

"Can you believe it?" Jack gestured at the crush of onlookers. "They're *fans.*" He shook his head in bemused wonder. "We're taking turns deciding who to let in for the service. Christ. It's like trying to get into a trendy disco." He shook his head again. "Unbelievable. You'd better get in, there can't be many seats left."

The room set aside for the mourners was adequately large, and ventilated, if not air-conditioned. I spotted Barry in the third row from the front and squeezed my way through the people blocking the aisles. When he saw me, he moved over, squishing Lissa and David Ogden sitting in the same pew to his left. Leave it to Barry to find a way to sit next to Lissa. Just as I was settled, Sal Steinbeck materialized and horsed his way into the six pew-inches on my right. One of the strangers at the far end of the bench, to the left of Ogden, yielded to the compression and stood next to the wall.

Steinbeck nodded solemnly to us all sharing the limited seating, and patted my uppermost thigh in sympathy.

"You haven't called," he muttered, too close to my ear, and casually positioned his arm on the back of the pew, around my shoulders. Barry laid his hand on my knee. I reconsidered my earlier decision not to induce vomiting.

I leaned forward an inch and replied, "Neither have you."

"Busy," Sal said. "You know."

"Yeah, what with the grisly murder and all." I just didn't have it in me to be properly respectful.

Sal looked at me oddly and removed his arm. Barry lifted his hand from my knee. I felt terribly ill-bred, but a lot less claustrophobic.

I couldn't control myself and whispered to Barry, "Where's Elaine?"

"Police headquarters. She came in from the Island with Kendall's books. Your buddy Duchinski wanted to see them immediately."

"I'm sorry," I said insincerely, wondering if Barry had any idea that his girlfriend was ethical enough to throw him to the wolves, "but since she's so devastated, perhaps it's best that she's not here."

A clergyman appeared, giving Barry no chance to zing me back.

The service itself was as strangely pleasurable as show-business funerals can be. The eulogies lean toward the funny side; the music was performed by friends, and so better than usual; the minister appeared relatively irreverent, as expected; and there was lots and lots of hugging among relative strangers. Knowing that there would be press littering the street outside, there was also much primping among the mourners before exiting.

As a reflex cryer, my nose was very red from copious blowing. I knew it was shallow of me to notice, but my hair looked fine for a change. We all, shallow but polite, filed out in orderly fashion, pew by pew, into that damned sun.

I lit a cigarette within a foot of the door. Flash cameras were blasting at us under the entrance canopy, only because Lissa and David Ogden chose to tarry with me. Barry was lingering, too, looking profoundly morose. Lissa maneuvered me to her left, in order to present her best side to the paparazzi. I didn't mind, since, that morning, I didn't even know where I could rent a good side for myself.

When about eighty thousand pictures had been snapped, Sal took my arm and said, "I know a quiet place in the neighborhood," catching the others' eyes in invitation. "Let's blow this pop stand."

As, arm around me, Sal led the way, with the aid of the security contingent, through the fans and press, I caught sight of Jack. He was coming out of the chapel talking with Dana Fisher—who was all smiles, until she caught herself—and my very own cop, Sergeant Dan Duchinski. Extricating my right arm from Sal's grasp, I signaled Jack to follow. He shook his head, sorry. Dan glanced up, and I just had time to mouth precisely, "I hate you."

We entered the dark cool of my favorite Irish bar in New York, McAleer's. The incredibly handsome, very married bartender, Timmy, looked up and shouted as we entered, "Vic! Long time no see." He took in my black dress, and wittily added, "Where's the funeral?"

I winced and waved back. It wasn't Timmy's fault. He usually sees me in rehearsal togs—lots of torn spandex and baggy tops. It shouldn't surprise you to know that Timmy's an actor, too.

All bartenders in New York City are actors.

We all wandered to the back of the large room and settled at the round table in the corner near the end of the long bar and the jukebox, and cleverly out of striking distance from the professional-dart area. I noticed the bar had been recently painted: an unfortunate shade that reminded me of dried blood. There were splatters of the enamel speckling the 1920s marble-tile flooring. Three ceiling fans circulated the cool smoky air.

"What a nice memorial service," said Lissa. I agreed. David looked indifferent and Barry looked appalled.

Sal got up and said, "Irish coffee, all around, whaddya say?" He marched to the bar like a pro and placed the order. From the corner of my eye, I could see Timmy shaking Sal's hand and laughing. Sal must have told Timmy he was a producer, or Timmy would be swearing to God that McAleer's didn't serve Irish coffees. I've been a bartender. Coffee drinks are a pain in the butt to make.

While Sal waited at the bar, I sandwiched myself safely between Barry and Lissa. David Ogden pumped quarters into the jukebox, providing us with a long succession of Beatles songs, peppered by Jerry Lee Lewis and Jim Croce.

Against my better judgment, when the drinks arrived, I sipped at mine. To my utter amazement, it didn't kill me. I even had another during the obligatory reminiscing about Kendall. A few straggler fans had come into the bar on their way from standing vigil at the chapel. Straightforward gawkers were allowed to hang out and stare. Timmy, without being asked, threw out those who tried to talk with us.

"Helluva thing," Sal intoned. "A rotten shame."

Not that anyone would express the opposite position, but we all agreed.

"I just hope the police arrest someone soon," Barry said, not realizing how ironic his heartfelt wish was. "I was at headquarters all yesterday morning. Do you know how many billable hours that is?" he asked. "I don't know anything, for God's sake."

"Oh, Vic's on top of this," Lissa said. "We should all keep in touch with her to find out anything. Do you have any business cards, Vic?"

"Oh?" prodded Sal.

I wanted to be in Kuwait. Anywhere but in this conversation.

"How so?" asked Barry, giving me a dirty look.

"Oh, it's nothing," I muttered, not wanting to incur Barry's wrath by sharing info he wanted first, let alone suspicions he should *hear* first. "I have a friend in television news who kind of keeps me posted. So far, nothing much."

"Well, it's more than *we* know," said Lissa, including the rest of the group. "Vic must have ten pages of notes she got from Brad Sinclair yesterday. Those TV guys have a lot of sources."

"Not to mention your 'friend' Duchinski, the cop," Barry added bitchily to me.

Was it my imagination, or did Barry look tense? Could he be jealous? Or just worried?

Lissa stared at me. "You mean you know Duchinski, the man who was so mean to me?"

"You might say that," Barry intoned sarcastically.

"Why didn't you tell me, Vic?" Lissa was understandably aggrieved. "I thought we were friends."

I felt lower than a snake's belly. "I'm sorry, Liss, I don't know why I didn't tell you. We were probably being called to the set or something." I saw by her hurt expression I hadn't convinced her. "He probably wouldn't tell me anything, anyway." I could see that no one at the table bought that one, no matter how true.

"She's right, Liss," assisted Barry, "they don't *talk* much." Thank you, Mr. Right.

"Is Vic always so persistent, Barry?" Sal asked with a leer, never taking his eyes off me.

"Like a pit bull," Barry grumbled.

By the time our conversation finally turned to more upbeat subjects, Lissa and I had made our peace and switched to seltzer, the men to Jameson's whiskey, straight-up.

Sal and Barry did most of the talking, so, not shockingly, it was mostly business jammering. My concentration phased in and out. I wanted a nap. I wanted to forget that my husband just might be a killer.

"So"—Sal's voice cut into the background sound of Jim Croce's epic work, "Rapid Roy that Stocker Boy"—"I got on the horn this morning to California and told Olive, 'Get Tom. He's not doing anything right now.' "

"Tom?" asked Barry, riveted on Sal's every word.

"Selleck," Sal said, as though there were no other Tom in the world. "I said, 'Olive, let him know it would mean a lot to me personally.' But"—he held up his hand and indicated with a whirling gesture that he wanted another round—"just in case, we'd better start talking to Murphy and Chase."

"Brown and Manhattan?" I couldn't resist, even though I *really* wanted a nap.

Without taking a beat, Sal said, "Eddie and Chevy. Chevy's kind of old, I know, but I really liked what he did with that Fletch character, you know? I think we could really put these guys back on track."

I hadn't realized they'd been derailed. I wanted to ask how David's audition for Steinbeck had gone, but didn't dare. I figured I'd racked up enough animosity already.

Steinbeck's voice droned on and on, hypnotically. After what seemed a lifetime, Lissa stood and said she had to get home and study her lines. David Ogden, who I don't believe had said a word from the moment we'd arrived, grunted agreement, and the two "young folks" left together, muttering regrets. Barry checked his new Rolex and made a few urgent sounds. I was quiet, trying to decide whether to nap on top of or underneath the sheets. Sal ran his hand across my shoulders as he went to the bar to settle up with Timmy.

That woke me up.

"Walk me home, Barry," I whispered.

"You live twenty yards from here," he answered, looking at me as if I'd gone round the bend.

"I need a nap, Barry," I argued, finishing before he could waste more of our Steinbeck-less time, "and I *don't* want to take it with Sal."

Barry looked up. Sal was watching us and waved amiably. Barry waved back. I smiled. Sal turned back to Timmy.

"It's those short skirts you wear."

"Barry!"

"I mean it, Vic. If you'd wear slacks, this—"

"Barry," I said as Sal started his return to the table, "I'll give you the coffee grinder, anything you want, but just this once—"

"Ready?" Sal said, standing behind my chair.

"Ready," Barry said, standing. "Vic and I have some paperwork that really needs finishing." He pulled out my chair. "Hope you have some energy, Vic, because this stuff can't be put off any longer." Bless him, he scowled at me.

"Okay, okay," I grumped melodramatically, wanting to kiss his tie—or that warm place between his jawline and ear. I couldn't decide.

Sal hailed a cab right outside the pub door and headed for his hotel. Barry walked me the twenty yards to the stoop of my tenement, trying to be annoyed with me, but not really accomplishing it. At the foot of the stairs, I leaned against him. He ruffled my hair in the back and held me for a moment. In that instant, I made a conscious decision to believe in Barry's fundamental honesty. My unconscious decision was between me and my God.

"Thanks, Barry," I said, meaning it, my hand lingering on his chest.

"Forget it." He didn't move.

"Want to come in?" What was I saying?

"I ought to get home," he said.

"I owe you the coffee grinder." I smiled up at him.

"That's okay. Keep it." He didn't smile back, he just looked. "It's yours."

I didn't need to be hit over the head. "You got a new one." A statement, from me. No anger anymore, but my eyes filled with tears. Silly. It was just a coffee grinder.

"Yes, Vic," Barry confirmed not unkindly. "I got a new one."

78

I kissed him quickly and stumbled up the stairs. I didn't want to blot my eyes while he was watching, so it took a while to fit the key into the lock on the foyer door. I supposed I was still drunk, so I went directly to bed and fell asleep on top of the sheets, still wearing my special funeral dress.

After all, if it got ruined, I could just get another.

The nap didn't go well. I was awakened by the sound of the telephone at four in the afternoon. I didn't answer it, and let the answering machine pick up. No amount of rearranging myself could get me back to sleep, however, so I got up and threw some food in Slasher's bowl while the red light on the answering machine blinked accusingly at me.

The only technology I dislike more than the telephone is the answering machine. Because of this modern advance, I, like all New Yorkers, am forced to lie with some regularity and complain about the answering device being on the fritz. Otherwise, I would spend my life on my second-most-hated thing, the phone. People don't see one another in Manhattan, they just call. And call, and call. That's when they're not punching buttons.

I hit the "play messages" button. I washed my hands in the kitchen sink and splashed my face during the whirring, clicking, and beeping. As I dried my hands and peered into the refrigerator, the message played.

Beep! "Vic, if you're there, pick up." It was Frances James. I dropped the towel, let the fridge door close, and stood by the infernal machine. "In case you're there, I'll just keep ta—Vic, for God's sake, please be home. I need to talk to you. I'm at a pay phone and I don't know how long—" *Beep!*

So I was right, Frances was alive. Alive, but not sounding very good.

Beep! "Look, Vic, I guess you're not there, and this is my last quarter. God, I hope you call in for messages. I'm going to try and call you tonight around eight, if I can. Please, please be there. I need to—" *Beep!*

Damn, damn, damn. I must have slept through the first

call. I sat down on the kitchen floor, narrowly missing sitting in Slasher's decaying bowl of Tuna Delight. While there, I replayed the messages. Why didn't I take Barry's advice and get a new voice-activated machine that lets people talk as long as they want—like the one he took? Silly. Because I couldn't afford one. I ran through Frances's messages one more time to be certain there wasn't something I missed.

Not a thing.

I called Dan-the-rat's beeper, left my number and went to the bedroom to change out of my funeral dress.

I was struggling into my tightest jeans, Dan's favorites, when the phone rang again. I accidentally knocked Slasher off the windowsill getting to the receiver before the second ring.

"Hello?"

"No," Dan said flatly. From the background din, I thought he was calling from his office.

"You don't even know what I called about," I said, sounding as injured as a guilty person can manage.

"The answer is still no." I could hear Dan eating something. Potato chips, I think.

Our conversations were becoming as limited as Barry intimated, so to vary Dan's response and move the dialogue along, I resorted to everyone's favorite diversionary tactic— sex. "What if I said I wanted you naked in the worst way?" Which, as we all know, is in a BMT-line subway car.

"No." I heard papers being shuffled. Or maybe he was closing the bag of chips.

"No?" That was it. Time for me to retire from my short-lived career as a femme fatale.

"No," Dan said, "because I'm going to be working late. Sorry, babe."

"Oh," slipped out of my mouth before I could stifle the relieved tone. "But you have to eat!" Damn, an exclamation point had slipped in when I wasn't looking. I controlled myself. "How about dinner?" The pause told me he was thinking it over at least. "I'm buying."

"Well," Dan came back on line, "I guess I could get away for an hour. You'll have to come by the office, though."

"See you around five," I said. Perfect. Dan's office was exactly the place I most wanted to be. I kissed Slasher on the nose and barreled off to the subway, not quite understanding why Kendall's murder had become such an obsession—but admitting it was.

All the way downtown I knew, just *knew* something big was going to come out of this day. Proving that even passably psychic actresses can be incredible schmucks.

CHAPTER EIGHT

I took the Broadway local subway to Forty-second Street, Times Square, where I bumbled around, stupidly looking for any indication whatsoever that I could make a connection with the funky N train. After much bumbling, indeed, I finally broke down and asked an elegantly robed gentleman who was peddling incense in one of the walk tunnels where the hell I was. He said we were all on the road to damnation, and that I should follow the conga drum.

Sure enough, as the jungle percussion got louder, I was on the trail into the bowels of the BMT line of the New York City transit system. A steep ramp downhill into what felt like the molten center of the planet, and I was there. The conga player singing for his supper had attracted quite a large crowd, making it impossible to get anywhere near the rear of the platform, where I knew I *ought* to be. Still, the rhythm made the stifling wait less terminally wilting. Nonetheless, the train was most welcome when it finally arrived. Air-conditioning would have been even *more* welcome. Nine stops and six beggars later, I was in the judicial epicenter of Manhattan.

Dan's office building looked like an old abandoned "Kojak" set. That's probably why professional set designers get paid the big bucks: realism. The elevator was broken, as usual, so I dragged myself up three flights of curved marble stairs, which gave new meaning to the phrase "deferred maintenance."

Hunks of plaster were gouged from the stairwell walls, slathered entirely in Pepto-Bismol-pink semigloss. I'd thought it an odd decorator choice for a police building the first time I noticed it. When the temperature spirals over ninety in New York not much impresses me, except jogging actuaries.

I was panting like a hound in labor by the third floor. All the huge windows in the complex had been painted shut sometime in the 1920s, and the city was in a brownout, so there was no air-conditioning relief to be had. The internal temperature hovered around 95 degrees on the first floor and climbed right along with me. Intent upon twisting some information out of Dan, I dragged myself into the large room that served as office space for fifteen investigators.

In retrospect, I now know I should get a hobby to replace all this vicarious living, like rug hooking. At least I'd always be at home and armed with a sharp object.

My wheezing must have given me away, because without looking up at me, Dan said, "You should quit smoking."

His desk area was in the middle of the sea of desks, and not sure I could make it that far, I fell into a nauseatingly turquoise, molded-plastic seat near the door. While I concentrated on oxygenating my respiratory system, Dan spoke to the man at the desk nearest his own.

"Your girlfriend's here, Contigliozzi," he said, adding, "Don't tell her anything. It will only encourage her antisocial behavior."

I only had the energy to hold up my hand. Waving was temporarily out of the question. Giving Dan the finger was an option I rejected out of deference to my upbringing, and respect for cops in general.

Frank Contigliozzi's face lit up. He dashed from behind

his desk directly to the water cooler. He drew water into a mug emblazoned with the logo of the Federal Drug Enforcement Agency, and brought it to me.

"Sorry about my germs, Victoria," he said, looking at the mug, "the city wants us to conserve."

I smiled wanly, drained the cup, and thanked him.

"You look great, Tor-Tor," Frank commented sincerely.

"Watch it, Frank," Dan said from his desk, not meaning it.

Frank examined me for signs of fainting, which I no longer exhibited, and asked me sweetly, "Think you can make it to my desk?"

I nodded, still a little weak, and followed him to the center of the room. He pulled a chair over from a vacant desk and placed it between his and Dan's.

Lungs reinflated, I said, "Thanks, darlin'." I always call Frank "darlin." He's too young, too cute, and too nice for the likes of me. But he gives me hope for the future of the city. I was feeling much better.

Soon after, I was feeling much, much better. I was getting strong vibes from Dan, glowering away at his pile of papers. I knew he'd be hiding something from me, but my instincts told me he was hiding something *great.* After a tantalizing ten minutes, he stood up.

"I'll just go to the little boys' room, and we can go eat."

Even *better,* he was going to leave his desk in my dubious custody.

Grinning at me sweetly, Dan stacked the pile he'd been handling, evened the edges, and locked them with a flourish in his bottom drawer. He slapped me on the back and said, "Be right back!"

Call me hypersensitive: I guess I pretty much hated Dan's guts at that moment.

In aggravation, I leaned my elbow on Frank's desk, with my cheek on my hand, knocking a helter-skelter of materials to the floor. Pondering my next move, but compulsively neat, I picked the litter up piece by piece and put it back on the edge of the Contigliozzi work surface. The final—and heaviest—item I lifted from the gritty floor was a clear plastic bag filled with small change, three stray business cards, a matchbook, two rubber bands, and a set of keys.

I could have sworn the bag buzzed in my hand.

"What's this?" I asked Frank.

"Oh"—he glanced over—"personal effects." He took the bag from me. "Homicide." Frank put the bag on the opposite side of the desk. Realization hit him. "Oh, gosh, that's right. You—" He stopped himself.

"Kendall James," I finished the thought for him. "Yes, I did." I reached back over and grabbed the bag, holding it so the contents spread evenly over my palm. "Isn't this *interesting!*" Frank looked concerned, so I finished his next comment for him, as well, "I know these things might be clues, and shouldn't be handled outside of the bag."

Frank relaxed and started showing off. "That's right. That stuff was lying around James's body when he was found. We have quite a complex system for getting evidence from everyday objects such as these."

So did I. I moved my right hand slowly over the tops of the pocket droppings, waiting for I wasn't sure what.

"But don't these things belong in a pocket?" I asked, "What do you think they were doing on the floor?"

"Excellent question, Tor!" Frank was filled with enthusiasm, as well as a plethora of nicknames—some of which horrifingly ended in that "ee" sound—for me. He was trying to watch himself. "We figure the murderer must have rifled James's pockets after he killed him." Frank looked very wise and pleased with himself. "It's probably not what's *in* that bag, but what's *not* in it."

"Really?" I murmured, projecting great admiration.

Wham! There it was. The buzz—or whatever, words fail me a lot when it comes to how I get vibes—came from the set of keys. Frank and Dan were on the wrong track.

I'd found the murder weapon. Poison keys? Was it possible to forge metal with viable poison content? I didn't think so.

"No!" Dan said, coming up behind me and slapping my hand with the bag the way one slaps a recalcitrant dog's nose. I dropped it. "Frank, for Chrissakes," he growled, "can't you see she's too old for you? Get your hormones in line." Then, to me, he said, "Come on. You sure as hell owe me dinner now." Dan turned to Frank and said, "I'll be back within an hour. Don't give away my desk, okay?"

Dan grabbed my arm and hustled me out the door.

We went directly to the health-department hit-list of an Indian restaurant across the street. Dan chose the non-smoking section. He was in such a mood, I didn't argue. He gave the order to the waiter before we'd even sat down.

"If I had time, I'd make you buy at the Russian Tea Room. Boy, you piss me off." He stuck his hand in the air and said, "Can we have some water here?" Not through with being angry, he lectured me, "It's a damned good thing we already dusted that junk for prints. Boy," he repeated, "you can piss me off."

"I only touched the bag," I defended feebly. "I think I know something, Dan."

"How?" he said, nodding at the waiter with the water. "Through your 'psychic ability'?"

I believe my mouth fell open. I'm glad there wasn't any food in it yet. Dan and I never talked about my fortune-telling. I knew better than to share my "hunches" with a professional hunch-maker.

"My what?" I answered stupidly.

"Boy, I'm starved." Dan took pity on me, I suppose, because he went on, "You're in the file, Vic. You were at the party. There was a discussion among the principals on the subject, so we checked it out." The cheese-stuffed bread arrived, and Dan tore off a hunk with his teeth. "You're a pretty impressive lady, lady. Documented as psychically 'gifted' in junior high school by the University of Southern New England. I'm glad we don't play cards together."

He was making fun of me.

"Not much of a believer, are you?" I said, taking a piece of bread for myself.

"No." Dan chewed and checked his watch.

Was that all he could say? No? It felt as if I were dating my mother. Except my mother would have picked up the check.

"I think I know what the murder weapon was," I said, choosing to ignore Dan. "Take it for whatever you think it's worth."

His mouth was full, but he managed to make himself understood. "Okay. Shoot."

"The keys in the evidence bag."

"Pardon me?"

"You heard me. The keys in the evidence bag. Kendall's keys."

Dan's laughter bounced off the walls of the tiny restaurant. "Don't tell me. He *locked* himself to death. Or"—he looked into my eyes—"Kendall was bludgeoned to death by a blunt Medeco." Tears were running down his face.

The man needed sleep.

"Have you tested the keys for traces of poison?" I persisted calmly, considering how irritated I was. This reaction was not entirely unfamiliar to me.

Dan's laughter slowed, and he admitted, "No." I could see his mind working. "But there were absolutely no open cuts anywhere on the hands through which the poison could have been transmitted." He felt he had redeemed himself.

"What about his mouth?" I asked.

Dan looked at me as though I were the slowest woman he'd ever met, and said, "Of course it was by mouth. I was simply refuting your theory."

The food arrived, and it all looked like grass to me, so I took the last of the bread.

I continued reasonably, "Kendall was always putting things in his mouth. Everyone who knew him knew that. Do everyone a favor and have the keys analyzed."

"No. Let it go, Vic. We're pretty sure we know what happened and why."

"How? Who?"

"You know I can't tell you anything yet. Believe me, you'll hear all about it soon enough. Eat."

"I want to know."

"So, you're the psychic. Read my mind."

That did it. I had no reputation as "psychic to the stars" to protect, and was bored with badgering a stubborn cop. I watched Dan finish the meal, paid the check, overtipped—as ex-waitresses and -bartenders always do—vowed to convert to Catholicism and become the first nun-actress in history, and took the succession of subways back to the Upper West Side and the only dependable male in my life: Slasher.

The entire miserably hot trip was spent trying not to care how the rest of the investigation into Kendall's death went. But the minute I thought I was over it, considerations of Frances on the lam, Barry, Lissa, everyone who stood accused slapped at me. And then, there was that *very* bad feeling about David Ogden.

On the street, coming out of the subway station, I remembered the most important thing of all: that a man I had known and liked for over a decade had been murdered. That time, I didn't forgive myself for my shallow side. I was so preoccupied, it's a wonder my purse wasn't snatched.

Inside the foyer of my building, I could hear my frog-phone ringing. Gurgling, actually, which is how I knew it was mine. It stopped as I pushed open the door to my apartment.

My beautiful, antique-laden, ripped-apart apartment.

The glass-front oak bookcases had been emptied, books lying like broken dolls all over the celadon-green living-room rug. Papers, receipts and résumé shots had been ripped from my burled-walnut rolltop desk and peppered across the debris stew. Sofa cushions reclined against gaping drawers, as though sticking out their tongues at me.

"Slasher!" I called. "Slasher!" I fumbled through the mess and toward the back bedroom. Where was that damned cat? The bedroom looked every bit as bad as the rest of the apartment. In the hall closet, even *The New York Times* I used to line Slasher's litter pan had been pulled out and left on the floor.

The back window on the fire escape, the one the burglars *usually* use to relieve me of my excess upward mobility, was closed. The four-hundred-fifty-dollar decorator jailhouse-style bars, futilely installed and reinstalled and installed again to prevent these nasty little shocks, were intact. Breaking-and-entering criminals aren't the Einsteins of crime. That one window is the only one with a security gate at all. Go figure.

"Slasher! Dammit, Slasher!"

Not my cat! No one could be that horrible, to take my only loyal boyfriend. I envisioned finding his lifeless body beneath the debris. Tears ran down my face. "Slasher!"

With an energy I didn't know I possessed, I started throwing heavy drawers onto the relatively clear kitchen tiles, and then pawing through the piles of papers and books strewn in mountainous clumps. Ten minutes later, my boy was still missing. Feeling the pulse in my stomach pound like the congas in the subway, I then submitted to a frightening fit of unreserved hysteria.

Collapsed on the floor, back against the edge of the sofa, I sobbed, until gagging stopped me from hyperventilating myself into total unconsciousness. I threw my left arm over the seat of the couch, repositioning myself to continue crying when I heard the squeak.

I lifted the askew sofa cushion, and looked directly into the partially opened eyes of Slasher. He had slept through my entire mad scene. I turned, knees toward the dozing animal, and stared stupidly at him for five minutes, totally exhausted.

When the phone rang, I flinched so violently that the cushion thudded heavily back onto Slasher. He looked at me irritably, crawled from beneath the pillow, and ambled to the dining room table where he fell asleep again, zigzagged across several discarded Stephen King paperback novels.

Blub-blub-blub. The phone gurgled again.

Not now, I thought numbly. I have to call the police now. I answered it anyway, mostly because I'm a creature of habit, even when in shock. I reached up from where I remained kneeling in front of my chintz sofa, and lifted the noisome plastic frog body. The eyes lit up with each ring, and I flipped down the back legs, presenting the mouthpiece at lip-level.

"Hello?" I said, not sounding like me, even to me.

"Vic?" the female voice asked.

"Frances!" I sat upright and cracked my back against the edge of the Victorian coffee table. "Where are you, Frances? Everyone is frantic." I tucked the frog under my chin, rearranged one cushion on the sofa platform, and sat.

"I'm upstate, Vic, at a resort," she said quickly, "but I'm coming into the city tomorrow. I need to talk to you."

"Well, everyone needs to talk to *you.*" I pawed around, looking for my dropped purse and my cigarettes. I couldn't locate it or them. "When did you leave? Why did you leave?"

Frances interrupted me. "I'll tell you all about it tomorrow. Please say you can," she pleaded.

"Well, I'm not due on the set until two . . ."

"Wonderful!" Frances breathed in relief. "I'll come to you. Meet me at the Boat Basin at ten."

"Frances," I began.

"I've got to go, Vic. Thank you, thank you. You're the only person I can talk to right now," she said just as she hung up.

I was too weirded out by the monstrous disorder of my apartment to dwell on the peculiarities of Frances's condition or location, so I called the police. Cleverly, after the last break-in, I had the number entered on my autodial.

After twenty-two rings—yes, I counted—the connection was made, and the pre-recorded message droned on, telling me all lines were busy and I should stay on the line. I checked my watch.

New Yorkers take a perverse pleasure in noting precisely how much time they spend in line—that's "on line" for the natives—or on hold. At least, I appreciated, no genius had provided Muzak for the wait. Two minutes went by. I thought a few choruses of "I Love New York" would have been a funny touch, though. Another two minutes dragged by. Slasher was snoring up a storm; I could hear him from fifteen feet away. I gazed at the TV, wishing the phone cord reached far enough for me to turn it on.

That's when it hit me.

My television was still plunked heavily on the walnut sideboard opposite the sofa. The boom box was on its side, but definitely still under the long table. When I stood to look down the hall toward the bedroom, I could make out the contour of my jewelry chest on the bed.

Now, no New Yorker with any love of personal possessions would keep the good stuff where it's easy to get at. Decent necklaces and such are squirreled away in unlikely places so the robbers have to work for their ill-gotten gains. Nevertheless, burglars always, always grab the entire jewelry case on the off-chance they lucked on to a stupid victim.

I would check more closely after I got off the phone, but as far as I could see, nothing was missing. I hadn't caught the bad guys in the act: the window gate was intact, other windows closed, and in my search for the narcoleptic Slasher I had been through the entire apartment. There was no one else in the place.

Would someone trash my apartment for fun? Doubtful. Not that it doesn't happen—it does—but a friend to whom it did happen had the rare privilege of scraping graffiti and human excrement off her walls, too. Vandalism for its own sake is more imaginative in Manhattan. New York is a city of excess.

I was so deep in thought, I didn't immediately respond to the masculine voice that came on the phone.

"Twentieth Precinct, Jackson speaking," he repeated.

"Oh, hi," I said. Hi? You'd think I'd be used to talking to cops after Dan and my victimization track record. "Hello," I amended. "I just got home, and my apartment's been broken into."

91

"Name and address," Jackson asked in a monotone. I gave him the information. He went on, "Make a list of the missing items and file them at the precinct. If you're upset, you can call the Victims' Hotline; number's in the book. Anything else?"

"Well, that's just it," I said, plenty upset. "Nothing seems to be missing. I haven't had a chance to really go through everything, but it all seems to be here." I waited for an expression of interest. Getting none, I went on. "Should I leave everything as it is until you guys get here?"

"Just make a list of any missing items and file them at the precinct. You'll need documentation for your taxes," Jackson droned on, no doubt bored out of his mind.

I gave up trying to impress him with the oddity of my personal break-in and said, "When will the fingerprint team be getting here, do you have any idea?"

"Oh, we don't do that anymore."

"Excuse me?" I said politely before I stopped myself.

"We don't have time to investigate or prosecute common burglaries. I could send someone over, if you'd feel better, but he'll just make a mess."

Make a mess? No time to investigate or prosecute? When did I enter the Twilight Zone? And the final indignity: *common?* I was, yes, speechless.

Jackson spoke again, "If there's nothing else we can do for you Ms., uh, Boeing, I advise you to call the Victims' Hotline. The number is in the book." Then, without a pause, "Thanks for calling," and the disconnect click.

Terrific. Thanks for calling, indeed.

Someone had tossed my apartment, looking for something—and it wasn't a VCR. I plucked a gold chain I'd thrown into the candy dish on the coffee table and fingered it thoughtfully. This was not the result of some deprived person's drug habit.

I put the chaos back into some order, wanting the whole time to call Barry, knowing the time for that had finally ended.

With good sense unnatural to me even under normal

circumstances, I wanted neither Brad nor Dan around for artificial comfort. Straightening the three-and-one-half rooms took two hours, which I also used for some heavy-duty thinking. And my thoughts always came around to Kendall. So much for my decision to keep my nose out of the whole mess. Whether I liked it or not, I was up to my olfactory nerves in murder.

Absolutely nothing was missing from my apartment that I could see. In the immortal words of Lewis Carroll, "Curiouser and curiouser . . ."

Finally exhausted from the shock and my "neatness attack," I fell asleep, somewhere down the Upper West Side rabbit hole.

CHAPTER
NINE

N ot surprisingly, I awoke early with a start, feeling as
if I'd been clubbed. Indirect light swept through the crack
between the plank shutters barricading the back bedroom
window. Since that's as much illumination as my boudoir ever
receives, I had to check the clock for actual human time. Early
enough.

I walked directly west from my building, crossing the
honky-tonk of Broadway, then smug West End, and finally
the placid, east-side-of-the-street-only Riverside Drive.
Rather than meander around the footpath into Riverside
Park, I swung my legs over the four-foot stone wall and
dropped wearily, pointed in the right direction. Clumps of
spring bulbs slumped beneath cherry trees, and beside metal-
grate trash cans. Large dogs illegally bounded ahead of their
masters.

I got to the Boat Basin at Seventy-ninth Street and the
Hudson River a half hour ahead of schedule, and perched
myself on the high rock wall overlooking the houseboats and

yachts. The New Jersey skyline—yes, there is one—glinted from across the water. Riverside Park was still dozing, with just the chirruping of sparrows and cooing of pigeons as background music. The shock of the previous evening's invasion faded in the soft sunlight. Maybe I was just tired.

The fact was, I was balanced on a man-made precipice, thirty feet above the oily pavement below, waiting for a woman who was the prime suspect in a homicide investigation. I checked my watch and swung my feet, knowing that Frances James had always leaned toward the unstable side. She was the kind of woman that even large dogs watch from the corners of their eyes.

Suddenly, fearful of heights, I swiveled and jumped backward from where my legs had been dangling, and, feet planted firmly on the ground, leaned with relief against the cool stones, fascinated with the slowly swishing water and the bump-bump-bump of the boats against the dock.

"Vic," Frances said from just behind me, "I'm so glad you're early."

I twirled so quickly around to face her that I scraped a large patch of skin off the inside of my right arm on the rough granite. Frances looked worse than my abraded skin felt. She wore no makeup at all, and her hair was flat, mouse-brown, hanging limply over her ears.

Frances ran at me as though propelled from a slingshot. I braced myself, not trusting myself to judge the motivation for her enthusiasm. I took a surreptitious peek over the wall, judging the distance to the hard cement.

At least I was waking up.

"Vic!" Frances said, hugging me. "Oh, thank you for meeting me. I really didn't know what else to do. You always have an answer. You have your power."

I felt very stupid, and certainly without power. Holding her back away from me, so WASP, so New Hampshire, I told her it was nothing. Longer sentences were being put off until I got my heart out of my throat and back down under my Maidenform where it belonged.

95

Luckily, Frances was in a talking mood.

"Let's walk, Vic. I feel so exposed here." Frances took my arm and pulled me to the right and down the stairs toward the waterside walkway. The forsythia were blooming, I noticed. "Did you bring your cards, Vic?" she asked.

I must have looked at her blankly, because she just continued talking.

"What am I going to do, Vic?" she asked plaintively.

"Can we sit, Frances? I'm not feeling all that well." I pointed out a bench under a well-leafed oak tree, and maneuvered her into a sitting position. "First of all, where have you been all this time?"

"At the Squamtawk Inn," she answered, as though it were the most reasonable place in the world to be while her husband was being memorialized. "I saw Kendall's service on the news. Was it nice?"

"Very nice. Now, why were you at the Squamtawk Inn instead of at the service? Everyone is very worried about you, you know."

"Oh, I'll bet," she said, uncharacteristically sarcastic. "I'll just *bet*. When Kendall was around, I never even existed, and now people are *missing* me."

Rather than tell her that wasn't true, I lit a cigarette.

"I wish I knew who did it," Frances went on calmly. "Who killed Kendall, I mean. His dying makes everything even worse than it was."

"How bad was it, Frances?" I asked.

"He was cheating on me," she answered. "Just look at my palm. I know you saw it when you told my fortune." She held her hand in front of my face. Rather than check the lines, I held it and listened. "He was always cheating on me," Frances continued weakly. "Now I know I'm not beautiful—I never have been—I wasn't when we got married." She plucked some lint off her cornflower-blue slacks. "And Kendall was very beautiful. I used to watch him as he slept, and wonder why he ever married me. I still don't know."

"Maybe he loved you," I offered.

96

She snorted what might have been a laugh. "Oh, yes, Kendall was *full* of love. He spread it everywhere." She looked at me forgivingly. "But you knew that, didn't you?" She sighed and didn't wait for my response. "That's why I left the party and went directly to the inn. I was sick to death of his 'all-encompassing' love. The last thing I wanted to do was watch him sleep, looking so beautiful, again."

"You went directly from the party to the inn? How did you get there?"

"Rented a car. 'The city never sleeps,' you know. Actually, I was a little surprised they let me have a car." Conspiratorially, she whispered, "I was a little drunk." She was watching a fat chipmunk digging in last year's leaves. "I couldn't stand to be in a room with the person who arranged Kendall's little 'trysts.' Tell Barry I'm sorry for leaving so abruptly, will you?"

I said I would. Frances was rambling. It was to be expected, after all. I steered her back to the subject. "So you didn't see Kendall again after you left the party."

"No," she said, "I *told* you that. I went straight to the car-rental place on Seventy-sixth Street, and then drove to the inn."

Some bit of trivia was lost in my memory bank, but I couldn't put my finger on it. I asked, "Why didn't you come back when you heard Kendall was dead?"

"Don't be silly, Vic," she reasoned. "Kendall hadn't been sick. Lead actors have to submit to full physicals when they sign prime-time contracts. I knew he'd have to have been murdered. The police would ask me all sorts of questions." Tears welled in her eyes. "I just couldn't face answering them. All those affairs, right under my nose. And then that last one, worst of all. You just know it's going to be in all the tabloids."

I handed her a tissue. I knew how hard it was to lose a husband to another woman. To another man? Unimaginable. Then, knowing full well the reaction I would get, I told her, "The police need to question all the suspects, Frances."

"What?" She stood and took a step backward, away from me. "You don't mean they think *I* could have done it?"

It was clear in that instant that Frances didn't even realize she was suspected of poisoning her own husband. Even if I weren't getting "those feelings" that she was innocent, her reaction would have convinced me. I took her hand again, ostensibly to reseat her, actually to focus in on something that was bothering me.

Given the puckish come-and-go of my ability, I got nothing, except that Frances did not murder Kendall.

"I guess I should think about turning myself in, shouldn't I?" Frances asked.

"Perhaps you should," I agreed. "Would you like me to go with you?"

"Well," she said, looking at me as though I'd lost my mind, "I'm not going to do it *now*. I have to think. I'll call you when I've made up my mind."

"But Frances . . ."

"Next time, remember to bring the tarot," she said, walking off in the direction of the park exit and Riverside Drive. "Promise me, Vic."

"I promise," I said, wishing I could predict coming events the way I was given credit for doing. I almost followed, but caught myself. How deep did I actually want to be in this whole mess?

I finished my cigarette, more confused than ever.

I was early, too, for my call on the set of "Raging Passions," so I went directly to wardrobe, had my outfit okayed for the third time, and then to Lissa's dressing room. I guess I was on a roll.

As I passed the extras' room, the large guy with the tattoos yelled, "Hey, you Bowering?"

I peeked in, no longer positive whether admitting to my identity was a good thing, even on home turf.

"You," Mr. Tattoo said. "Are you Bowering?"

What the hell. I said, "Yes."

"You're wanted on the set. Pronto!"

"Thanks," said my lips, but my brain was screaming, oh, God, what now?

I was sick of the elevator and took the stairs down to the studio. Everything seemed calm enough when I walked onto the set. Lissa was lying on the dry, paint-splattered floor, going over her lines. Olive and Jack were making notes on a script behind the camera setups. Olive motioned me over.

"You called?" I asked her.

"Your lucky day." Olive smiled. "We just bumped you up to an under-five."

"Here are your pages," Jack said, handing me a one-inch-thick stack. "You're in scene twenty-three, your blocking doesn't change."

What blocking? I was standing behind the bar. Stage-hands had even marked the exact spot with a slash of masking tape with my character's name—barmaid—scrawled in magic marker. I wasn't likely to wander out of frame. Quickly I paged to scene 23, looking for lines marked "Barmaid." The anticipation was exciting, I don't mind telling you. Any urge I had to share having seen Frances earlier was swept from my limited mind like so much dust.

"Listen up, people . . ." came a female voice. I folded over the corner of the page I was on, and looked up to see Dana Fisher standing on the set.

"All right, everybody," Jack bellowed into my previously good ear, "*Listen up!*" I guess he wanted to get Dana over with as soon as possible. She nodded at him royally.

"I just wanted to let you all know how much I, as the producer and creator of this show, appreciate how hard you've all been working. The writers have been at it night and day, revising the story line, and, I think, have come up with a winner.

"Since Kendall's unfortunate exit, viewership is way, way up. And I think, with your continued loyalty and diligence, 'Raging Passions' is going to continue to add fans, until"— Dana paused dramatically—"we are the *number-one show on daytime!*" Actors, being great audiences, broke into applause. Dana waited until just the right moment, and resumed, "We owe it to our fans, to ourselves, and—most of all—to Kendall! Now, let's get it in the can!"

The set went wild. I wondered when Dana was going to get to "the Gipper" part.

"You know," Olive said next to me, "if I were casting a megalomaniacal producer, I would settle for no one less than Dana. I don't think I've ever seen anyone so thrilled over the sudden death of another human being." She jotted something on a script, and amended, "Or actor." She handed the papers to Jack, who wandered away.

"She did look pleased, didn't she?" I agreed.

"Want some coffee?" Olive asked, and walked to the giant urn at the back of the soundstage. She handed me a cup and poured one for herself. "This business sucks, sometimes. I really loved Kendall, despite that 'SPA!' business. I hate the mileage Dana's getting out of his murder."

"What 'SPA!' business?" I asked.

"Oh, you know." My face said I didn't, so she explained, "My not wanting him to do 'SPA!' It wasn't anything personal; Kendall was, in my not-so-humble opinion, just too damned old for the role. I was talking to one of Marty Sheen's boys—I mean, we're talking box office here. We were right down to it, too. One minute Sal is tickled to death, and the next he won't have any actor but Kendall." She shook her head. "I must be getting old myself. I don't get it."

Jack shouted, "All right, everybody on the set for scene twenty-three. Let's block this sucker."

Ten minutes later, having memorized my critical line, "Another, sir?" I was lying on Lissa's dressing-room floor, eating a Snickers bar and contemplating the ceiling. I was about to suck the chocolate off my fingers and go call Dan to tell him about my mystery break-in, when Sal Steinbeck walked in, and over my prone body.

"Nice," he oozed.

I sat up.

"Hear you bagged an under-five. Congrats," he said, pouring himself some coffee from Lissa's thermos. "Lissa still on the set?" I nodded. "Well," he said and sipped, "I'll catch her later." As though I cared, he continued, "Have a meeting with Ogden this morning. We're shooting location footage for 'SPA!' next week, and word is Ogden's getting deep-sixed from 'RP.' Though he could use some work. He can't act his way out of a paper bag, but he's pretty." He poured more coffee. "That's show biz."

"Sure is," I grunted as I stood. "Well, I'd better go study my line. I'll tell Lissa you stopped by."

"You know, Vic, there's a role in 'SPA!' you'd be really good for. Has Olive spoken to you about it?"

I know what you're thinking. God knows, I was thinking it.

"No, actually," I said, as transparent as Sal.

"Well, that's funny."

Har-de-har-har.

"She's been pretty busy." I could play the game.

"Look," he said, draining his cup, "I have a cast breakdown. Why don't we have dinner tonight and talk about it?"

Sal had pulled out all the stops. Dangling a possible acting job *and* a free meal before my eyes. I was not exactly putty in his hands, but certainly Play-Doh at his dinner table.

"Terrific," I accepted, knowing much, much better. "What time?"

"Pick you up at eight." He walked past me to the door, without touching me somewhere for the first time in memory. "Hi, Liss. How you doing?" he said, running into Lissa in the hall. She answered something curt and squeezed past him into the room.

"What a slime," Lissa said, closing the door. "Don't sleep with him. It's not necessary."

"I wasn't going to," I answered.

"So what do you think of the latest?" Lissa asked me.

"What latest?"

"The police picked up Frances for questioning this morning. Didn't Barry tell you?"

Of course he didn't. Neither did Dan, or Brad. No wonder I love my cat.

I wanted to tell Lissa about my meeting with Frances, and the destruction of my apartment, but stopped myself. I just didn't know whom to trust anymore.

It was time to exercise a little discretion. It was too late, of course, but I didn't know that then.

Blahhhhhht.

Sal rang my buzzer precisely at eight. He hit the button too hard and way too long. That should have been my first clue. He didn't bring flowers. That should have been my second. But all was forgotten when he led me to his limousine.

Since it was a Mercedes, I overlooked the fact that it was white. To my great disappointment, the only neighbors on the street to appreciate my upward mobility were the two Chinese ladies who lived upstairs. No doubt about it, they were beginning to consider me pretty damned hot.

"Any particular place you'd like to eat?" Sal said as the chauffeur closed the door.

I wanted to say I'd been craving McNuggets, but stifled myself. "What do you suggest?" I asked instead.

Cars with televisions always provoke that David Niven speech pattern in me. Car phones used to, but I got over it.

"World Trade Center," he told his driver. "Champagne?" Sal offered. It was Moët & Chandon, so, against my better judgment, I nodded.

The trip to the southern tip of Manhattan was filled with Sal's dropping of every name in the entertainment business. We hurled down the West Side Highway, past meat-packing warehouses, punk and gay bars, scattered gas stations, and auto-body shops. Cannibalized carcasses of deserted cars littered the potholed thruway at frighteningly regular intervals. Illegal gypsy cabs cut lefts across two lanes of traffic. From time to time, we pulled out of the passing lane to the right to allow screaming ambulances and fire trucks access. I concentrated on developing an Emma Peel persona to replace the late Mr. Niven in protecting me from the smarmy Mr. Steinbeck. By the time we arrived at the World Trade Center, I pretty much had it down pat.

My ears popped twice during the elevator ride up to the restaurant, which offered a nosebleed-elevation view of Manhattan. After the eatery's initial opening, I hadn't realized that anyone but tourists frequented the place. Sal's accent was definitively "New Yawk," and the maître d' greeted him by name, so I guess I was wrong again.

We were seated at a table for four, directly against the glass wall, fifteen feet from the excellent piano player. I'll admit it; I was impressed. New York City restaurant tables are generally so small, you have to put your wineglass on the floor when the food arrives. We actually had elbow room—in the smoking section, no less.

Sal went straightaway to the piano player, dropped a profoundly new-money fifty-dollar bill in the brandy snifter atop the baby grand, and made a request. Upon his return, he moved the chair to my right smack against the arm of my chair, and slung his arm around the back.

"I ordered up some show music," he said, "thought you'd like that. Am I right?"

I hate the question "Am I right?" nearly as much as I loathe show music. Unless it's Sondheim—either asking or playing. The evening was already shaping up into a confirmation of my earlier actress/nun impulse. The opening strains of "Can't Say No" filled the room. The piano player winked at me.

"Perfect," New Hampshire me answered, very much missing the company of my cat. Sal snapped his fingers for the waiter. I cringed.

I've been a waitress, and I know what the staff can do to the food of customers who annoy them. Visine is not just for bloodshot eyes, I can tell you.

"Champagne, you pick, oysters half-shell for me, seafood

103

ravioli for the little lady," Sal said as I shrunk down into my chair, befitting a "little" lady, "and the Chateaubriand for two." He flipped the menu over his shoulder at the waiter, who walked away, hating both our guts.

"That okay for you?" Sal asked me as though it mattered to him either way.

"Perfect," I answered with a vapid smile.

"I was a waiter once." Sal grabbed a roll and ripped it apart. "Shitty job. I worked a lot of shitty jobs to get where I am now." I did my part and appeared interested. That's all it took with Sal. "Grew up in the Bronx. The Bronx! After I got out of the Navy, I took any job I could get, so I could get the hell out. I had these ideas, you know? Like I couldn't stop them. I'd be repossessing a car or something, and I'd be thinking, Hey, this is really *interesting,* you know? This would make a great series. Or I'd be making deliveries for Greenberg's Pharmacy, and I'd still be thinking, What if Greenberg's was a front for a major drug cartel? So every night I'd go home and write down these great ideas. Didn't take too long before I was on my *way.*"

The champagne arrived, Dom Perignon, and Sal waved the waiter away without tasting the sample. He filled my glass, and continued. "I'm telling you, you wouldn't believe the stuff I've done."

This was undeniably true. I took a sip of wine.

"Good stuff, huh?"

Another one of those "Tell me I'm right" questions.

"Perfect," I answered.

"I probably shouldn't say this," Sal began, as I silently agreed that whatever it was, he probably *shouldn't* be saying it, "but when I found out you used to be married to Barry, well, you could have knocked me over with a feather. I mean, a terrific looker like you. Well, you know. When Kendall told me you two were quits, I thought to myself, Sal, this one's for you. This woman deserves the best!"

"Well, that's very sweet," I said à la Niven, having forgotten Emma Peel entirely in the torrent of self-aggrandizement slopping over the table. "You must miss Kendall. Even besides the problem with the series."

"There's no problem with the series," Sal responded, shoving another piece of bread in his mouth. "I mean, sure I miss the guy, but 'SPA!' is a hell of a project. We're gonna lose some big bucks at the start, what with losing time with recasting. Maybe hundreds of thousands, but we'll get anybody we want for this baby, sooner or later."

"I'm sure. But Frances did mention how closely you and Kendall were working on the show."

I have no idea why I said that. Frances had said nothing of the sort. The words just sort of fell out of my mouth.

"When did you talk to Frances?" Sal asked through a mouthful of baguette. "I mean, isn't she in police custody? That's what David Ogden told me."

"Yeah, I heard that, too, but I met her before she turned herself in."

"No kidding? I didn't know you two were that close. I mean, I know she thinks you can predict everything down to a stock-market crash, but the last I saw of her, she was hell-bent on having it out with Ken—*mano a mano,* so to speak."

"Did she say that when you took her home after the party?" I asked. Something was hinky here, but what?

"Sure did."

"But she left town."

"Sure did. Don't know if she offed him and ran or what. That's what most people would do. Am I right, or what?"

I put a ravioli in my mouth to avoid having to answer that.

"Well," Sal continued, "I got her out of that damned party. Who could have known what she had in mind, huh?"

I popped another pasta, and thought. Frances had told me she went directly from the party to the car-rental place. I felt sure she'd told me the truth. Of course she'd been distraught. Frazzled, I reminded myself, but innocent. Yet, I'd misinterpreted so many things lately, how could I be certain of anything?

105

How do judges make these decisions day after day?

"Personally, I wish I'd never taken her home. I should have made her come back to my hotel with me." Sal slurped down an oyster, whole. "The Plaza, you know."

I was saved by the arrival of the Chateaubriand, which was wonderful. Sal ate with the enthusiasm of a trucker who had another five hundred miles to cover. I passed on dessert, but succumbed to the cognac.

"So, enough about history. Let's talk about you," Sal said. "Exactly what is your availability?"

Yes, he meant both kinds.

"Aside from reporting to Twentieth Street and Sixth every Tuesday at eleven for unemployment, my schedule's pretty free." The cognac was the cocktail straw that had broken the camel's back. Obviously, I will never learn.

"You should get Barry, the man, to up your alimony. Happens all the time. He looks like he's got the bucks."

"I didn't ask for alimony," I admitted for the millionth time since our separation.

Sal's face broke into a huge grin of total disbelief. "You're kidding! Where have you been all my life?"

I sank into my chair. This kind of embarrassment would never have happened to Ivana Trump. Sal signaled for the check and said, "Let's go up to the observation deck." He threw four fifty-dollar bills on the table and grabbed my arm. I smiled apologetically at the waiter, hoping the tip was adequate.

The observation deck was nearly deserted—not much of a surprise, given the late hour. The wind nearly knocked me over as we stepped out onto the concrete. It felt as if my hair was going to be pulled out at the roots.

"Is this great?" Sal asked another non-question in the still ninety-plus temperature.

"Perfect," I shouted over the whining wind.

I then knew what the view is like from the inside of a convection oven. But this was, ha-ha, business, I thought.

"Look at that!" Sal yelled, hustling me to one corner of

the deck. "That's Ellis Island! That's where my family entered America." He put his heavy arm around my shoulders again, and pointed way over to the southwest. The only thing I could make out was the Statue of Liberty. I leaned out farther.

You guessed it.

The Bowering luck—the karma of one foot in the grave and the other in Arab territory—kicked in at precisely the moment that my entire body weight was balanced on the ball of my right foot, and at the same time I felt a ferocious blast of wind from below. With the bulk of my torso serving as a giant tarp, I was lifted a full foot from the flooring. My center of gravity shifted in a second, and I could feel my feet flipping upward and behind, forcing my upper body over the rail. The flailing of my arms only propelled me farther forward.

I have never in my life been more certain I was going to die—with the possible exception of the night when I was shoved onstage to perform in George Bernard Shaw's *Misalliance* on three hours' notice and no rehearsal.

You're going to have to trust me here. One hundred twenty-two stories is very high up, even after a brief ricochet off the "safety" platform too many feet below. Especially in the dark.

I felt my knees breaking.

In fact, Sal had hurled himself at me and caught my old basketball injury in an enthusiastic tackle. We thunked to the ground, bones rattling, and my head making a rather spectacular clunk. We lay there for some moments. The thudding of my heart, and the rasping of my breath, all but drowned out the murderous wind.

"Holy shit," was all I could finally manage. Sal's chest was heaving, and for a moment I was afraid he'd have a coronary there atop the World Trade Center.

"Are you all right, Sal?" I asked, once I'd determined that, against all odds, I had not wet myself.

"Well, whaddya know?" he muttered, standing and inspecting his Italian suit. "Reflex action. *Bam!* I had ya, just like *that.*"

I tried to get up, but the trick knee buckled, and I fell stupidly again to the floor. Sal grabbed me around the chest and pulled me up and walked me back to the elevator.

"How 'bout that?" Sal asked more to himself than to me, over and over, all the way to the lobby. "Sons-o'-bitches architects should have thought of that wind shit," he said to me once we reached the relative safety of the street.

"If you hadn't grabbed me, I would be splattered from here to Herald Square, Sal," I said, outside the revolving door. "Thanks."

"Hey," Sal answered, crooking his head to one side coyly. "Anytime. Let's get you in the car. I don't know about you, but I could use another drink, and there's a bottle of twelve-year-old Scotch in the bar in the back."

"Sounds good to me," I said, as he propped me against a wall and went to peer around corners in search of his driver.

"Look," Sal said as he walked toward me, "I've got that script at the hotel. You could clean up a little, take a look at it, and we could talk."

I finally understood what it meant to be a real person, and not an actor. I wanted a long bath; I wanted to empty my bladder; I wanted to take a Valium. Maybe two Valiums. And, at that minute, I wanted them all much, much more than I wanted a stupid bit part on a stupid television show. So much more, in fact, that just as I was about to cut off my nose to spite my face and ask Sal if he was *crazy,* I started to cry.

There was much starting of sentences, and stopping to blubber. By the time the hiccups started, Sal had gotten the message that this might not be the perfect night to slam "Bolero" on the old stereo and light some candles.

"You gonna be all right?" Sal asked.

I made a few more whimpery noises.

Sal considered. "You don't look so good to me." Understatement of the week. "I know a quiet little joint with booths in SoHo—real close. After you have a brandy there, maybe you'll feel more human. Whaddya say?"

Being incapable of speaking, I had finally devolved into

the perfect woman for Sal. He got me into the limousine, and after a short drive, out again and into the promised booth. Ever the vain actor, I creaked up out of the seat and went to the ladies' room to repair my face. In the unmerciful light of "Les Femmes," I settled for simply wiping off the raccoon eyes my mascara had left under my lower lashes. It was not a big accomplishment, considering how long it took me.

Sal pushed a large balloon snifter toward the wall, got up to allow me to sit, and then slid his body next to mine in the enclosed space. I felt as though I had been buried with an unloved relative, but concentrated on the brandy.

"Better?" Sal asked. I smiled feebly; he put his arm around me. I didn't have the resources to wince. "That's right, just drink up." He babbled pleasantly until the liquor was gone, and ordered another for me. His knee accidentally brushed mine forty or fifty times while he talked about his billions of projects, and how at least thirty-three million of them were just perfect for my obvious talents. I finished my second drink in silence.

"So, you up to looking at the script I was talking about?"

My eyelids fluttered sleepily. "No," I answered. I was pleased at rediscovering my verbal skills—however limited they had become.

"Sure, sure, sure," he commiserated. "You're still shook up, huh?"

"Huh?"

"Okay," Sal continued compassionately, "look, I've got some stuff to take care of. My driver'll take you home and I'll just catch a cab, okay?"

I believe I nodded. "Okay."

Sal plunked me in the back seat of the limo, told the driver to take me home, and closed the door behind me. He was walking away before we pulled away from the curb.

I knew I was in shock on the trip back to my neighborhood, because I only gave two or three contemptuous thoughts to the miserable lack of chivalry in New York men. Otherwise, the thirty minutes' travel was a blur. I was out of the limo and at the outer door of my building before the driver had a chance to get out and escort me. I did remember to wave him away while I dug in my purse for my keys.

It took a while, since, out of old habit, the keys were already in my left hand.

My knee was throbbing. Twice, I tried to get the wrong key to open the vestibule entrance. When I heard the opening click at long last, I checked behind me—again out of habit, to be sure no bad guy was going to push me in and commit bodily injury upon my shaken person. The street was quiet. Billy, the attendant at the parking garage across the street, was sound asleep in the brightly lit entrance. As I pushed open the door, I noticed that my right shoulder was badly bruised. The twenty feet to my door seemed endless as I hobbled toward home.

I was thinking how awful it was to get old and infirm when I was grabbed by the arm and twirled off to my right, ricocheting off a sharp corner and into the solid body of a large man.

He had hidden himself in the two-foot-square cubby behind the stairwell door leading to the commercial basement space. The Bowering luck being what it is, he jerked violently at my brand-new bruise, trying to cover my mouth with his hand. Ever the lady, I instinctively shouted.

"Shit!"

The man slammed me against the wall, whacking the breath from my lungs, and smashing my head hard enough against the poster I'd hung to relieve the tenement gloom to shatter the glass. My bottom hit heavily in the shards, and I cut the palms of both my hands.

"Shit! Shit!" I yelled. Not very imaginative, I know, but spoken from the heart.

Moronically, I was more irritated than frightened; my brain was so filled with disaster for one evening that it was rejecting the new.

The man pulled me to my feet by my hair, and I *made* room in my overtaxed cerebrum for real terror. This hulk was trying to kill me *now*. Never mind the staggering sum of eleven dollars in my wallet. I was going to die: not as Czarina of all the Russians or in the arms of a twenty-year-old boy, but in an extraordinarily tacky tenement hallway under bad fluorescent lighting. I struck at my attacker's head with my fingernails, aiming for the eyeball. He caught my hand before it got even close.

This time, I could only *think*, "Shit." The malevolent mugger's other hand had cut off my air supply, and my good knee was giving out right along with the bad one.

I wondered who would feed Slasher when I was dead.

"What ees this here?"

I was dropped like a one-hundred-thirty-pound bad habit to the tiled floor. I had a great view of two enormous sneakers. One of them kicked me. I didn't feel it. The sneakers streaked off toward the exit.

Two smaller sneakers appeared, and hands wrapped around my bruised arm, raising me upward. At half-mast, I recognized my superintendent, Carlotta.

"What za hell?" she asked, supporting me to my door. She pulled her keyes from her apron and tripped the lock. "Goddammit men," Carlotta grunted, propelling me toward the sofa. "Only ones t'any goot are cats." She picked up Slasher. "I wait. You call cops." She scrutinized the mess that was me, and finished, "Never mind. I call." She dropped the cat and started toward the phone. That snapped me out of it.

I didn't want a cop.

I wanted Dan, *my* cop.

CHAPTER
TEN

Carlotta sat with me for the half hour it took Dan to arrive. I can't remember what we talked about. Of course, I can rarely make out the mishmash of Italian/Spanish/English that Carlotta rattles off at lightning speed. I believe she was ranting about the bad manners of men, but I wasn't paying all that much attention to her. It seemed I was utterly transfixed by the panoramic view from my living room window of my next-door neighbor's living room window, interrupted only by fleeting thoughts of how badly the wilting pink-and-white impatiens in my window box needed water.

Carlotta rummaged around under my sink until she came up with a bottle of Courvoisier. She poured mine neat, and mixed hers with Diet Coke. That's the sort of thing that's hard to forget. When Dan rang the buzzer, Carlotta let him in.

She scrutinized him, and demanded (I think) to see his identification as a policeman. Unconvinced, she flipped open his jacket and checked out his pistol. As I tried to communicate my faith in Dan as a protector and fine human being,

Carlotta dropped to her knees and patted down his legs. She grunted once, picked up her glass of cognac and Coke, and walked out.

"What was that about?" I asked Dan.

"She was making sure I was carrying two pieces." He lifted the leg of his jeans, revealing another holster and what looked to me to be a 25-caliber.

Fifteen years in America hadn't taught Carlotta much English, but she had obviously learned more street sense than I had.

"Come here, baby," Dan said, holding out his arms for me.

That did it. Just that much sympathy and a pair of great, strong arms, and I fell to pieces. He held me close and walked me back to the couch. Once seated, I succumbed to a full five minutes of sobbing and shuddering. Dan rocked me as I watered his chest. Softly, over and over, he repeated, "It's all right now, baby. It's okay."

When I'd run out of tears, I said, "It was like he was waiting for me, Dan. My God, he was waiting for *me*. He never even made a grab for my purse. I don't understand."

"Things don't always make sense, babe. Trust me."

"But why? I need to know why," I persisted. "I didn't get the chance to tell you, but my apartment was tossed yesterday."

"What? Why didn't you call me?"

"Don't yell at me, Dan. Maybe you were too busy with Kendall's murder case," I accused. The look in his eyes affirmed my guess, but I was too happy to have him with me to hold a grudge. "Besides, nothing was missing. I didn't know it meant anything at the time. Now, I think it does. I think that man out there is part of it."

"I don't know," Dan answered. "But he *was* waiting for you. I checked out the space where he was hiding. There are only two apartments at this end of the hall. Your next-door neighbor is out of town for the summer—obviously, because there are about forty Chinese-restaurant menus stuck under the door. That cubbyhole isn't big enough for anyone to just hang out there on the off-chance someone might wander by." He gently wiped away the moisture on my cheeks. "Now, do you have any idea why someone would want to hurt you?"

"You mean kill me, don't you?" I asked, very much afraid of the answer.

"Yes," Dan said, "kill you."

I think I clutched Dan so hard when the phone fired off that I hurt him. He grimaced and disentangled himself very kindly. "I'll get it," he said in a voice designed to settle down the most psychotic of street people.

"Let it ring."

"Vic, it's nearly midnight. It's probably important."

"It might be that man," I cringed. My eyes filled with tears again.

"Exactly." Dan kissed my nose. "That's why I should get it." He stood and walked around me to get the phone on my right. I noticed his limp was better.

"Bowering residence, Duchinski speaking." Slasher jumped up on the telephone table and walked across the Touch-Tone buttons to get to Dan. Dan chucked him under one arm, and continued. "Sorry. May I help you?" It was clear that the caller wasn't my assailant. I shook my head to indicate how very little I wanted to talk with anyone at that moment no matter who it was. Dan nodded his understanding. "Vic has met with an accident and can't come to the phone," he went on. "No, she's all right, just a little shaken." He listened for a moment. "I think that's a very good idea. We'll be over in an hour. Yes, I have the address." He hung up.

"We'll what? I don't want to go anywhere, Dan. Please, just stay here with me and Slasher tonight."

"Don't you want to know who that was?" Dan asked.

"No," I answered. "Yes." I changed my mind. "But I still don't want to go anywhere. For God's sake, Dan . . ."

"That was Frances James. She's been released from custody and wants to talk to you. I want to talk to her, and you're not spending the night here, anyway. Go wash up."

"I will not leave Slasher in this—"

"I'll put Slasher in his carry-case. You go wash up."

"You still think Frances is a murderer, don't you?" I asked him.

"No."

"No? Then why are we going over there? Look at me. If I had any self-respect, I'd be a blithering idiot," I argued.

"I have my reasons. No, I have no intention of telling you what they are. Go wash your face."

For once, I was too tired to argue further and did as I was told. Dan's car was parked directly in front of my building. Illegally. Dan carefully positioned Slasher in his case on the back seat, as I climbed into the front passenger seat.

"Buckle up," Dan instructed. He tossed a deck of tarot cards in my lap and started the engine.

Dan's face was illuminated in the glow from the light over the tenement entrance. I'd never seen him genuinely grim before. I ran my hand over the stubble on his cheek.

"You had me followed. That's how you got Frances," I stated, knowing I was right.

"Bingo." Dan put the red Toyota in gear. "Give the little lady a stuffed animal." We pulled out into traffic, heading across Central Park at Eighty-first Street, toward the East Side and Frances's co-op. There was a line of depressingly young people milling around the entrance to McAleer's, no doubt a spillover from the half dozen in places in the neighborhood. No wonder beers had recently been upped to two bucks a pop. I put my hand over Dan's on the gear shift. "Wanna fight about it?" he asked with a smirk designed to put shaken victims at ease.

"With an armed man? How crazy do you think I am?"

"Very," Dan said.

"You have a suspect, don't you?"

Dan heaved a tremendous sigh. I prepared myself for a lecture, but all I got from him was, "Yes, Vic. I do."

That was the scariest part of his answer: the compliance.

We pulled up in front of the forty-story James co-op building and parked in a restricted zone. Dan flipped his windshield visor down, exposing a sign proclaiming, "Official Police Business." He stopped me as I was about to get out on my side.

"Now listen to me for a change," he said. He slipped an anti-theft device over the steering wheel and locked it. "You have been hell-bent to get yourself into the middle of this murder mess. Well, now you're here. I think Frances is bad news. I don't think she actually killed her husband, but I *don't* know what her involvement is. Your job for tonight is to tell her damned fortune and act like you just fell down the stairs or something. No talk about your attack, comprende?" I nodded. He continued, "I'm along to listen and make sure nothing lethal is slipped into your Perrier, okay?" He slipped his keys into his pocket and tripped the automatic door locks. "Okay?"

"Okay," I agreed. Dan carried Slasher in his traveling wicker. Into the lobby, past the doorman, and up a flight of stairs, my mind raced.

Someone was definitely trying to kill me. I accepted that as fact. Probably the person responsible for ransacking my apartment. But what was he looking for? Since my greatest claim to fame was an unflagging curiosity coupled with a minor intuitive gift, whoever my pursuer was believed that I had the capacity to psychically conjure up damning evidence. To some degree or another, that included everyone I knew, except Dan.

But who believed in me the most? Barry, who had nothing to gain from Kendall's death; Brad, who could not care less and had only met Kendall once; and Frances.

Dan is no dummy. It was also a fact that Frances had been free when I was attacked. She had had the time to arrange everything. She was also unaccounted for during the period in which my apartment was ransacked. And, as Jewel so firmly asserted, poison is a woman's weapon.

I was glad Dan was carrying two guns.

116

*　*　*

Frances opened her door immediately. For a woman who had spent most of the day in a New York City jail, she looked incredibly perky. A flush of color splashed across her cheeks, and the reddish face-lift lines I'd noticed at Barry's party had all but miraculously disappeared.

I limped into the co-op first, Dan and Slasher after me.

"Oh, good," Frances said, embracing me, "you brought a cat!" She closed the door and followed us into her white-on-white living room. Dan set down the wicker case, and Frances peered in.

"What does he do?" Frances asked me.

"Do?"

Personally, I've never known cats to do much of anything.

"Psychically. You must have brought him along for a reason. To enhance your powers? Of course." She beamed.

Well, if she wanted to believe that, it was just as well. Dan had told me not to mention my near fatality. I smiled. My face felt as if it was going to crack wide open. Obviously, I'd taken a good shot in the kisser that I didn't even remember.

"Can I get you a drink? You look a bit ragged." Understatement of the year. "I'm having one," Frances said, holding up her glass for emphasis. "Sit down, sit down. What would you like?"

"Wild Turkey, neat," I answered, lowering myself gingerly into a Haitian cotton chair. I hurt myself anyway.

"Nothing for me, thanks," Dan said. He stuck his fingers through the grating at the front of Slasher's case and wiggled them. I heard the cat's vigorous snoring.

Frances mixed herself another drink, poured my bourbon and plunked herself next to Dan on the sofa. Reaching over to get my glass from the coffee table sent shock waves of pain through my bruised shoulder.

"Thank you, Sergeant, for bringing Vic over." Frances leaned toward me, and patted Dan's knee. "Sergeant Duchinski and I had quite an afternoon, didn't we?" She patted his

117

knee again. I figured our hostess was on about her fifth vodka tonic of the evening, and was holding no grudges. "Are you two friends, or were you interrogating Vic when I called?" she inquired pleasantly.

The woman was amazing. She was chatting as though we were sitting at a faculty tea.

"We're friends," Dan said.

"Well, that makes me feel so much better." She smiled at me. "The sergeant asked me about a million questions, and I had the feeling that he already knew the answers. I guess I was right! Maybe I'm getting just a little psychic myself. Is that possible?"

Dan shot me a look, amiable face nodding. Whoever said I won't take direction?

"Of course it is," I agreed, tilting my head toward Dan. "I didn't know that Sergeant Duchinski talked with you."

"Oh my, yes," Frances said. "He was the first policeman I spoke with." She put her glass down on the end table. "After the one who read me my rights, of course. It was very interesting. Nothing like 'Hill Street Blues' at all. Can I get you another drink?" she asked, getting up and going back to the bar. I shook my head no. "They were all so certain I killed my husband. No one even asked me who else might have wanted to do it."

"Were there other people?" I asked. Dan got up and walked to the window facing out onto Central Park. "Kendall was always so sweet."

Frances laughed sharply. "Yes. Sweet. Well, not everyone thought so. *I* didn't think so.

"Kendall used people the way most people use chopsticks. Yes, he was a sweetie. He screwed everyone in sight— literally and figuratively." She toasted nothing in particular, and went back to her seat on the couch. "He fucked 'em all. Everyone on 'Raging Passions' got left high and dry with no notice. Dana would have probably lost control of the show; Jack would have gone in a heartbeat; so many soaps are shot in California now, not one in four of the actors were going to

118

have jobs to go to. Then, of course, there are the people who *really* wanted Kendall dead."

Frances apparently found the idea most amusing. She chuckled into her glass, giving her voice a hollow other-world quality. "Oh, Kendall deserved it, all right. Now"—she changed gears and sat upright—"do my cards, Vic. Let me know what happens to the little wifey-boo. Am I going to rot in jail? Live happily ever after? Which? Maybe the spirits will reveal the murderer to you. Who knows?" She giggled again, tickled at her own wit.

I looked over to Dan, still standing, gazing out at the view. He nodded casually. Frances had forgotten he was even in the room. She was drunk enough; she probably wasn't even aware of what room she was in. I pulled the cards out of my purse and started shuffling. I had a sick feeling in my stomach that this operation was going to go entirely too well for my taste.

"Do you have a candle, Frances?" I asked. "White is best."

"Oh, of course," she answered, "I'm sure I have some in the kitchen. How many do you need?"

"One, two, it's hard to tell. Bring me as many as you can find."

"Be right back," Frances said over her shoulder on her way to the kitchen. I dashed at a frustratingly slow rate over to Dan.

"Dan, what do you want me to do here?"

"You're the psychic. What do you think?" he whispered.

"Get her talking. Get her agreeing. Keep her forgetting that you're even here?"

"Bingo. Not bad, Bowering. Now, get back there." Dan pointed to my seat, and made himself as unobtrusive as a 240-pound man can, just as I resettled and Frances bustled back into the living room.

"I found three," she said. "I hope that's enough."

"That's fine," I said, lighting the candles, and moving the shuffled tarot deck back and forth over the open flames.

119

I don't have a clue why I—and many other fortune-tellers—do this. It's supposed to purify the cards, and it feels right, so what the hell.

"Now, Frances, cut the cards three times and leave them in separate piles. All the while, concentrate on the question you most want answered."

When she was through cutting, I put the piles together and started laying out the Celtic Cross, a divination method of which I am especially fond.

"Are you concentrating?" I asked her, while part of me was hoping she wasn't.

Frances closed her eyes and nodded affirmation.

Wham!

I got it. As clearly as if she had said it aloud, I knew that plain, sad, widowed Frances had a lover. And not anyone Byronesque—a hot, steamy stud muffin. This emergency reading wasn't about Kendall's death. It was about Frances's life—with another man. Every presumption I'd made of Frances's innocence was suddenly suspect. I tried my best to keep my expression bland.

"The first card is your significator." I flipped the card over.

It was La Mort. Death. But the death card is most often interpreted not as the end, but as rebirth.

"New beginnings," I said aloud. "Covering you is . . . Duperie, deception." I laid the card directly over the first. Frances looked pale. I continued, "But since the card is covering your significator, it is protection. Any deception here is a good thing."

"Go on." Frances appeared instantly sober.

"Crossing you is"—I turned over another card, and laid it sideways over the second—"Espérance, your wishes. What were you wishing for, Frances? What dreams could hurt you?"

"Go on." Frances drained her glass without answering, but stayed where she was sitting.

"Your crown is . . . Repentance, repenting; your ability to take responsibility makes you special." Frances just stared, so

I went on, laying the crown above the cross, and another below. "Basic to the question is Mensonge. Lies."

Dan turned around and faced into the room. Frances murmured something so quietly I couldn't make it out, and started rocking.

"Do you know what that means, Frances?" I asked her. She rocked harder and looked utterly miserable. I saw guilt. But inside I saw something else, something Frances was not aware of. I saw lies told to her, still unrevealed. My worst fears were being realized: I was on a roll.

I went on, "Near past is Colère, anger—not yours, someone else's. A man's anger at another man. Near future"—I laid another card to the right of the cross—"is Misère, poverty; again, not yours." I looked closely at Frances's face. She knew exactly what I was talking about then. She believed the poverty card, but it surprised her. Why? "All right," I said, "the last four cards leading to culmination are, let's see . . . Égarement, confusion; Inquiétude, anxiety; Pleurs, sorrow; and Veuvage, widowhood." It was a classic positioning of the cards, but it was up to me to give a credible interpretation. I have always believed that the cards appear at random—only the skill of the reader makes a decent reading.

After a moment of waiting, Frances said, "But I *am* a widow. How can the end card be widowhood, when it's already happened?"

"I don't know, Frances. You'll have to give me a minute."

This situation was a fine example of why I quit the fortune-telling biz.

What I saw I could not, in good conscience, tell. So my job became the construction of a fine lie that could be backed up by the illustrated cardboard laid out in front of us. Poor Frances, the ultimate believer, was watching me with frightened rabbit eyes, terrified of what I might tell her. The cards weren't exactly depictions of carnivals and domestic bliss.

"I've got it!" I said, triumphantly, I hoped. "All these cards refer to a period of mourning. You are a widow already, but will need to go through a period of adjustment—confusion, anxiety, sorrow—to come to terms with your loss." I could see she needed more. Fortunately, I had a truth available for disclosure. "There is absolutely nothing in the cards to indicate prison, or even trial." I looked up to see Dan glowering. I think he would have smacked me himself if he'd been closer. I'd deal with him in the car, when we were alone.

"Really, Vic? You're not just lying to make me feel better, are you?" Frances asked.

"Look at the cards," I sidestepped neatly. "Do you see anything that even remotely suggests imprisonment or legalities?"

"No. No, I don't. But what was all that about an angry man?"

Oh, what a tangled web we weave . . . In my own defense, I was sooooo tired.

"That's the other one who cares for you." Oops.

"What do you mean, Vic?"

I backpedaled furiously, "That's the *good* news. There's another man who waits for you. I don't know for sure, but I'll bet that's where his anger comes from. Waiting. He probably accounts for the lies in the cards, too. He's trying to keep his affection a secret." Clever, huh?

Not at all. The minute I said it, I knew it to be true. At least almost true. I was so terribly, miserably tired, and the whole psychic gimcrack only seems to work when I don't try or don't care.

"Oh, thank you, Vic. Thank you, I feel so much better." Frances was glowing again. Whoever this mystery lover was, he made her happy. I thought maybe, at long last, I could just curl up with Dan and fall hard asleep, but Frances's gratitude knew no bounds. Her voice cut through my lethargy.

"Let me find my checkbook. I want to give you something for all your trouble, and don't you dare tell me you won't take it!" Frances bounced up and over to the sleek white bentwood desk on the wall behind us.

"Really, Frances," I protested feebly. The sentence was

spoken mostly to get me to a warm bed. Money is *always* nice.

"I know what it's like to be struggling." She rifled through the papers stuck in layered cubbies. "I know it's here. It has to be here. Kendall was an absolute fanatic about keeping the checkbook up-to-date and . . . Well, that's strange. It's not here."

"Maybe Kendall had it on him," I offered.

"No," Dan spoke up, "it wasn't among his personal effects."

"No," added Frances, "we had a rule that the checkbook never left the apartment. If either of us needed a check, we tore one out and took it with us. *Never* the checkbook." I could see the panic rising in Frances. Not chagrin or confusion, but panic. She averted her eyes. "Well, never mind. It'll turn up, and when it does, I'll send you a little something, Vic."

What was going on here?

"I know you must be tired, Mrs. James," Dan said from near the window. I'd even forgotten he was there. "We'll be going now." He hefted Slasher's carrier, grasped me by that damned injured arm again, and led me toward the door. "We'll be in touch."

Frances waved from her position by the desk as Dan closed the door. I threw an arm over Dan's broad shoulders and let him carry the majority of my weight—not to mention Slasher—to the car. I was gritting my teeth against the pain, and so didn't have much to say until we were all ensconced in the little red Toyota.

"What was that quick exit about, Dan?" I asked.

"I don't know what you mean."

"Yes, you do. When Frances couldn't find that checkbook, you did everything but carry me out." I crossed my arms stubbornly, knowing Dan wouldn't start the car until I'd buckled up.

"There have been some financial irregularities. Happy? Now buckle up."

"I *guessed* that. What aren't you telling me?"

"Did anyone ever tell you you're a pain in the ass?" Dan asked belligerently.

"Yes. You did, and more than once."

"What about your husband, Barry?"

"Him, too." I knew, in that moment, we were talking about more than Barry's spousal irritation with me. "What about Barry? Dan, dammit, I'm too beat up to solve riddles. Talk to me, Dan."

"When we demanded Barry's records of transactions made for Kendall James, your husband asserted that they were missing."

"Asserted? Asserted? You're saying you don't believe the records are missing at all. Dan, why would Barry ditch Kendall's financial records?"

"Why, indeed? Now buckle up."

"I wish you'd stop lying to me. It's very annoying."

"You lied to Frances," Dan said, securing his seat belt and pointing at mine. "Don't be so imperious."

"Who said I lied?" I answered, knowing he was right about the imperious part.

"I said. Anyone in the world could have seen it."

"Well, Frances didn't. And"—I turned to him—"just who the hell is the psychic around here anyway?"

"Good question. We'll talk about that tomorrow. Right now, I'm taking you and"—Dan inclined his head toward the back seat and Slasher—"the boy home with me. This whole mess is getting nasty and, God knows why, I'd like to see you survive it."

Dan reached for the ignition key. I reached over and put my hand tightly over his. Something was coming to me.

"What?" Dan asked.

"Shhh. I'm thinking."

"Well, that's a first." He tried to pull my fingers away.

"No. Not yet." I had the overwhelming sense that the evening was far from over.

"What?"

"Just wait," I whispered, "something's going to happen."

"What?"

"I don't *know*. Just trust me; it won't be long."

And it wasn't. Within the minute, Frances appeared in the light of the entrance to her building. She said something to her doorman, who stepped to the curb.

Dan leaned forward for a clearer view, "What's she up to now?" he asked.

The doorman hailed a cab. Frances thanked him and got in.

"She's going to see her lover!"

"Her what? My God, don't you show-biz people ever rest?"

"Look who's complaining."

That explained Frances's plastic surgery and glow all right. What do some women do when their husbands are cheating? They cheat right back. My gut told me I knew the man, too, and that he had been at Barry's party. Jack? No. Sal? Yuck, no. Who?

The cab pulled away from the curb and headed downtown. I revived from my reverie and smacked Dan on the arm, "Well, *follow* her. What's the matter with you? I thought you wanted to solve this case. What kind of a defender of the people are you anyway?"

"You'd better be right, Vic."

"I am," I said with the confidence of a habitually determined woman in possession of no proof whatsoever. For every hundred times I question a feeling, there is that one shining insight I would bet my life on. This was one of those.

It wouldn't bother me to be half right so much if, when I'm wrong, I weren't so horribly, inextricably half wrong.

CHAPTER ELEVEN

Follow that cab. I can't believe I'm doing this," Dan was muttering to himself. "Follow that cab. I'm trapped in a Sam Spade movie."

We were headed down Fifth Avenue. Traffic was mercifully light—which would mean heavy outside of New York. Cabs cut in and out of lanes like crazed hummingbirds, barely missing us. Befuddled New Jersey drivers clogged intersections and tried to enter one-way streets the wrong way. That was our good luck. Frances's driver was a pro, running red lights and narrowly missing both pedestrians and buses alike, but even he had to slow down for a good old New York gridlock. The only reason we didn't lose him entirely was because the cab was an old Checker, and bigger than the sea of yellow whizzing before us.

I caught sight of the illuminated spires of the Empire State and Chrysler buildings. Dan was right: we were both trapped in a Bogart/Bacall film, only with dirty streets.

They turned left on Forty-second Street, then headed

south on Second Avenue, and pulled up in front of a huge complex of white brick—gone Manhattan-gray—on the north side of Twenty-third. Dan idled on the east side of Second Avenue, and watched the building.

"Ogden's place," Dan said to himself.

"David Ogden?" I was stunned. "But I was so sure Frances was meeting her lover." How could I have misjudged so badly? It had been, after all, one of those *shining* insights.

Not taking his eyes from Frances as she exited the cab and walked into the tremendous chandeliered lobby, Dan asked me, "And you're not sure now?"

"Well . . . no."

"No?" Dan shifted into first gear and pulled away from the curb. "No, she says." He neatly cut over three lanes of traffic without turning a hair. "And why not, if I may ask?" Dan briskly maneuvered the car into the circular drive in front of Ogden's building.

"David's gay," I said, embarrassed at my conclusion that Frances was racing around in the middle of the night in search of a little physical comfort.

"Gay?"

"Queer as a football bat," I winced. "Lissa told me the first day on the set."

"Well, no one told *me*," Dan grumped, shutting off the engine. "*I* was told that he and Lissa were engaged. *I* was told we went on this merry chase to nail the lover of a homicide suspect. *I*, apparently, am never going to learn." He unbuckled, pocketed the keys, and opened his door.

"What are you doing?" I asked.

"Since we're here, don't you think it would be swell to find out why Frances is paying a call to a homosexual associate of her dead husband's in the dead of the night?" Dan easily heaved Slasher's case out of the back seat and slammed the Toyota door. I struggled out of my restraint and—with some difficulty—the car.

"I admitted I must be wrong. Are you doing this just to humiliate me?" I whined, trying not to.

127

"No," Dan said, barreling through the entrance, careful not to knock Slasher on the entrance door frame, "I'm doing this to humiliate *me*."

I hobbled as best I could behind him, as the concierge charged forward to confront the annoyed battleship of a cop.

"There's no standing in the driveway, mister," the uniformed East Indian ordered. I admired his pluckiness.

Dan flipped his gold shield at the man without a word and started toward the elevator bank. The concierge blandly went back to his station and his early edition of the *New York Post*. No doubt, he'd seen—or read—it all before.

Dan suddenly turned mid-march, almost knocking me over, and strode back to the reception desk.

"Here," Dan said, thrusting the cat carrier at the concierge, "guard this with your life." The man nodded, looking very blasé indeed, as though such things happened every night. Dan continued, "What apartment was the woman who just came in here going to?"

"Thirteen-ten," came the response, "That's Mr.—"

"Ogden's," Dan said. "Thanks."

I barely made it into the elevator before the doors closed. When the doors opened on the thirteenth floor, Dan spoke again.

"Guess Ogden's not the superstitious type."

The fact is, *all* actors are the superstitious type. After the week I'd had, being on the thirteenth floor felt like a brazen tempting of fate.

There was a sign pointing to the left for apartments 1301 through 1330. Without pausing, Dan turned toward 1310. He was most emphatically pissed off with poor bruised me. I took Dan by the elbow to make him slow down. He stopped.

"I'm sorry, Dan," I said. He raised his eyes skyward, a vision of long-suffering acceptance.

"It's okay."

"What are we going to do when we get there?" I asked.

"Nothing much we can do. We don't have cause to enter. Wait a while, I guess. Maybe listen at the keyhole." I think he felt sorry for me, because he added, "You're not crazy, Vic. Something's going on. I just don't think we're going to be able to—"

Frances's screams cut the tranquil air of the peach-and-celery-colored hall. One scream followed another until they became one long, undulating trill.

Dan streaked off toward the sound, pulling his gun from his shoulder holster. By the time I'd gimped to Ogden's apartment door, it was open, and Frances was sobbing into Dan's chest. Her keening was punctuated irregularly by throaty growls emanating from somewhere deep in her chest. It was horrible to hear.

Trancelike, I walked to the bedroom at the rear of the apartment. Lying like a broken doll was Ogden. The beige carpet was sodden with blood. As I got closer, I could hear a soft rhythmic squishing with each step. My shoes made pale prints in the blood-saturated wall-to-wall carpeting. I have no idea how long I stood, looking at David's body, his blood soaking into the soles of my sandals. Dan's voice came to me from very far away.

"Vic!" he yelled. I don't know after how many tries. "Vic, get in here!"

I broke out of my fog, and hustled back to the living room, tracking crimson.

"Take off those shoes, Vic," Dan told me as I walked toward him, where he was holding Frances in the middle of the room. I meekly kicked the splattered white sandals off and went over to where the man and woman stood, tepee-like. "I have to call this in, and Mrs. James won't let go of me. Here"—he unwrapped Frances's arms from around him, plunking them on me. I cringed a bit with the pain from my earlier injuries, but managed to hold her upright. "Try not to touch anything, and keep her calm," he instructed. He dialed the precinct direct and gave our location. Frances suddenly dropped to the floor and grabbed her knees. I eased myself down to her side, very concerned that Frances was becoming catatonic. Dan made one more call, though I couldn't hear to whom. When he hung up the phone, I spoke.

"What happened, Dan?" I asked, rubbing Frances's heaving back in a slow, circular motion. I lowered my voice. "I mean, do you think Frances killed Ogden?"

"Nope," he said and rubbed his temples. "Too much blood soaked into the rug. The carotid arteries were severed—hell, it's a wonder his head is still attached at all." He paused during the ensuing shriek from Frances and, abashed, continued, "But Mrs. James hasn't been here long enough to have done it and have the body empty itself like that. I'd say it happened at least an hour ago."

Frances suddenly quieted.

"Is he going to be all right, Vic?" Frances asked pitifully.

As I searched my mind for an answer that wasn't a lie but not quite the truth either, Dan knelt beside us and said, very kindly, "I'm afraid he's dead, Mrs. James."

There was a pause in which Frances seemed to consider this strange turn of events. Her eyebrows furrowed slightly as she pondered. Then, with no warning, she scrambled to her feet so abruptly, I was flung to one side.

"No! No! No!" she screamed. Quick as a cat, Dan caught her in a bear hug, restraining her flailing arms. Her foot nearly took off my jaw when Dan wrestled her to the sofa.

"Why did you come here tonight, Mrs. James?" Dan asked firmly. "Why? Were you afraid something was going to happen to Mr. Ogden? Mrs. James, listen to me. If we are going to find out who did this, I have to ask you some questions, and I need them answered *now*."

With the word "now," Frances stopped her frantic motions as quickly as she'd started.

"What?" she asked Dan, looking as though she'd just seen him for the first time.

"Why did you come here tonight?"

"Oh!" Frances sat up straighter. "After you and Vic left, I went through the desk again looking for the checkbook. It

130

wasn't there. It is definitely missing." Her eyes were glazed and shifting rapidly from one object in the room to another.

Dan tried several times, and failed, to get her attention. He gestured for me to try.

"But why did you come here, Frances?" I asked.

"Oh!" she said again. "I thought David might have taken it."

"Why would he take the checkbook?" Dan asked. Frances continued looking at me.

"Why did you think David took the checkbook, Frances?" I asked once more for Dan.

"Because we were lovers, David and I."

I congratulated myself for having been right even when I thought I was wrong. But then, that left the gnarly question of whom Kendall had been sleeping with. Or had Ogden been having an affair with both of them? I went on without Dan's encouragement.

"But why would he take the checkbook?"

"I don't really know. I guess because I was always afraid that David didn't really love me. I *knew* he hated Kendall." Tears started running down her ravaged face. "I thought David killed Kendall. The two of them were working on some 'projects' for film development together. Then, all of a sudden, everything went sour. You know, somewhere in the back of my mind, I always thought David seduced me just to get back at Ken for something."

"For what?" asked Dan to no reaction.

"For what?" I repeated.

"I don't know. Some business thing. I don't know."

"But that still doesn't explain why you thought David took the checkbook, Frances," I cajoled. "What did you think?"

"That . . . that . . . I don't know . . . that David was blackmailing Kendall." Frances's voice picked up speed and volume. "I went through the bank statements for the last few months and there weren't any especially large checks written. There were none.

"I even checked to see if any extra-large deposits were made on the chance that Kendall was blackmailing David." Her chest heaved. "Kendall knew about David and me, you know. He knew, and he didn't care. The only thing he cared about was 'SPA!' It was all he lived for, that damned, stupid show."

At that moment all hell broke loose. Two paramedics appeared in the open doorway, followed by five uniformed and three plainclothes police.

"No!" Frances shrieked. "No, I didn't mean it. David didn't kill Kendall. *He didn't!* I won't let you take him away!" Her screaming turned to wails and babbling.

One paramedic went into the bedroom at Dan's direction, the other tried to subdue the now hysterical Frances. Dan finally lifted Frances from her feet, much the way he had earlier, and held her until the medic gave her an injection. She fell limp in his arms almost immediately. It was not until Dan laid Frances delicately on the sofa that I stood and wandered back to the doorway of the bedroom. The men were standing around. No doubt about it, Ogden was stone-cold dead.

Dan came up behind me and said, "Come on, now. We should get out of the way. I'll make my report in the morning. They're taking Frances to the hospital. I've asked for police surveillance. She'll be all right."

I didn't move.

"How was he killed?" I asked. "I know his throat was cut, but with what?"

"Razor blade," Dan answered, leading me toward the hall door.

"Cocaine," I said, not asking a question.

"Right," Dan said. "And there's something else I guess I should tell you. You've been through enough," he continued, moving me steadily nearer the paramedic who had sedated Frances. He spoke steadily, soothingly.

"Barry has been embezzling money from Kendall for years." I flinched at the words, but he didn't stop. "We're pretty certain your husband is the murderer. He should be in custody right about now." My eyes widened in disbelief. Dan held me upright, and nodded over my shoulder.

"And one for the little lady," he ordered the man in white.

I felt a jab in my arm and then nothing.

CHAPTER TWELVE

I awakened in my own bed.

Dan was lying next to me, fully clothed, with Slasher asleep between us. Every body part I owned was knotted; my tongue felt like the underside of a felled tree. My brain was trying to connect with my spinal cord and missing, so I lay there waiting for my bruised synapses to fire.

What was Dan doing in my bed? Aside from the fact that it broke one of my cardinal rules—no one spends the night— even if I'd broken it, why was he in his clothes?

A brain cell came to life. Dan refused to have a fully physical relationship with a technically married woman. Of course he *would* have his clothes on.

No. That wasn't the whole story. What was?

I got up and limped to the bathroom, ran the water into the tub, and brushed my teeth. Twice.

Submerged in the bubbles, my memory came back. The entire previous evening whacked at me in terrifying detail. I jumped painfully out of the bath, wrapped myself in a towel, and hobbled back to the bedroom. Dan was lying on the bed, eyes open.

"What the hell did you do to me last night?"

Dan stroked Slasher and said, "Nothing. I'm as pure as when you met me."

"Not funny, Duchinski. What was in that shot?"

"I don't know." He heaved himself upright, careful not to disturb the cat. "That is a medical question. How are you feeling, by the way?"

"Like shit," I answered, picking up a copy of *Bonfire of the Vanities* from the nightstand and throwing it at him.

"Watch the cat, Vic. Do you have a spare toothbrush?" Dan grazed past me and into the bathroom. I followed in a rage. At the bathroom, he said, "Do you *mind*?" and closed the door in my face.

Undeterred, I raised my decibel level, "The whole evening you knew that Barry was in jail and you didn't tell me. Didn't you think I'd want to know something like that? Dan? Dan, answer me!"

"Can't hear you!" his muffled voice answered. The toilet flushed, and the door opened. "A toothbrush?"

"I don't have a spare, and even if I did, I wouldn't let you use it." Dan shrugged and lifted my own white toothbrush from the black porcelain holder over the sink. He slathered on toothpaste and proceded to brush, as I fumed, "You don't seriously think that Barry has been trying to kill me? Anyway, the killer couldn't be Barry. Ogden was murdered while Barry was in police custody!" I was very proud of my deductive reasoning, given my barbiturate buzz.

"I had Barry picked up as soon as we found Ogden's body," Dan said, picking up the razor I used for my legs from the tub rail and soaping his face.

"Well," I dithered, "that doesn't prove anything."

"Barry was in the shower when they got him. What was he doing taking a shower at two A.M.?"

"He's very neat." Which was absolutely true. The feebleness of my argument made my heart sink. I watched wordlessly while Dan shaved. I had no idea what to do next. "Dan?" I began.

"No."

"Stop doing that! Look at the mess I'm in because you keep saying no before you even hear the question."

"The question," Dan said, toweling off his face, "is 'Can you see Barry and talk to him?' The answer is no. You are going to stay where I can find you until I am satisfied that we have the right person under wraps." He eased past me into the kitchen and started the coffee.

"Aha! Then you're *not* satisfied that Barry is the murderer."

"Oh, I'm satisfied. I just haven't proved it beyond a reasonable doubt. Listen to me, Vic; your husband has been stealing money from the first victim for a long time now. We have subpoenaed the books and our account people are looking them over right now. But that's just for show. The fact is, during interrogation, Elaine admitted that she'd been tracking the numbers for some time. She was so concerned about it, she even spoke to Kendall. Somehow, from the time Barry received the paychecks to when they were sent to her, money disappeared."

"Stuff like that happens," I argued.

"Sure it does. But consider this: In the last six months, Barry dumped his wife of ten years, bought a three-hundred-fifty-thousand-dollar co-op, and got real cozy with the only person who could catch him dipping into Kendall's well. What do *you* think?"

"I don't know what to think."

"Then consider this: Who had access to your apartment? I don't guess you had your locks changed after Barry moved out. I know you didn't, because he was in here heisting your coffee grinder and microwave."

"But—" I started.

"And there was no indication of breaking and entering either the night your apartment was trashed, or the night you were attacked. Someone used a key, both times. How does that sound to you?"

"Not too good," I admitted. "But how does that explain the missing checkbook?"

"They're going through Barry's apartment this morning. I figure it'll turn up there."

"What if it doesn't?"

"Then Barry dumped it. I sure as hell would. Now I've got to get downtown. I don't want you going anywhere alone, do you hear me? I don't know when Barry will be getting out. Chances are, he knows a lot of good lawyers."

I was thinking.

"Did you hear me?" he demanded.

"Yes, yes, I heard you. But I'm telling you, Dan—Barry is no murderer. I lived with him for ten years. I *slept* with him."

"And now you've slept with me, too," he said without humor. "That doesn't mean I won't use your toothbrush. Now I have to get out of here. I'm going to have a squad car keep tabs on the building. I want you to call a locksmith and have your locks changed. *All* of them. Understood?"

"You're wrong about this."

"*Understood?*"

"Yes."

Dan grabbed his jacket off a chair and rummaged in the pockets. He pulled a small cylinder from an inside flap. "Here," he said, handing it to me, "it's Mace. I want you to carry it with you, even if you're just going to the can. Okay?"

"I'll hurt myself."

"Well, you won't be the first, will you? Carry it." He kissed me gently and opened the door. "It's almost over, Vic, but you're going to have to trust me."

I watched my big old cop lumber to the entrance door, the Mace hanging from my fingers. I was on sensory overload. I wanted to be back in New Hampshire worrying about nothing more than the mosquito problem.

But I still had things to do.

137

When the coffee was ready, I sat down and dialed Jewel's phone number. She picked up on the seventeenth ring.

"This better be good," Jewel growled into the phone, still fuzzy with sleep.

"I have coffee, Jewel," I offered. "I'll bring you a present," I pleaded.

"Forget the present." Jewel softened immediately. "Just bring the coffee."

I thought I was doing just fine until I opened the door and laid eyes on Jewel. The sight of her beautiful, sympathetic face gave flow to a sea of weak tears. I put the full coffeepot on the floor, crawled next to her on the sofa, put my head on her ample chest, and whimpered like a three-year-old for a half hour. Jewel just held me and smoothed my hair. Mothering was what I needed, and what Jewel gave me. That's my life: my mother the stripper. But my other mother was in New Hampshire, blithely waiting for me to grow up and get a real job out of New York, and somewhere in America. Ultimately, I came up for air.

"Damn," I said, "now the coffee's cold."

"Just heat it up on the stove, darlin', and then you can tell me the problem."

How desperately I wanted there to be only *one* problem. When we had our coffees, I launched into everything that had happened since the time I'd last seen her: meeting Frances, the apartment break-in, the attack, Ogden's murder, and Barry's arrest. Jewel was unnaturally quiet throughout.

At last she said, "I guess perhaps we were wrong," and pulled Brad's bootleg newsroom notes from beneath a pile of jewelry cases on her telephone table. Jewel handed me the pages apologetically. "You left these here the other day."

"He didn't do it, Jewel. I know Barry's a shit, but he *couldn't* have murdered anyone." I noticed her dubious look. "Not even for money, Jewel."

"Did you tell that to Dan?"

138

"He didn't believe me."

"Why not?"

"It was quite a bit of money."

"Ah." That was all Jewel said, nothing more than "ah."

"You don't believe me either," I said dully, feeling a little betrayed.

"Honey," Jewel said, pouring us both some more coffee, "I believe *you*. I even believe *you* believe it. But I know you like my own daughter, and I know that you still love that crud. Even when you admit his faults, you love him too much to believe he's a bad person. Darlin', it's looking more and more like you're going to have to start accepting that loving someone doesn't make that person better than he is."

Tears starting spilling down my cheeks again, and I quietly conceded, "I know."

"Now, what you really need is some rest. You look like forty miles of trampled bear shit, love, and your body needs to heal. Dan is looking out after you, which makes me feel better. You lie down for a while, and if you're up to it later, I've got a nice bottle of Moët & Chandon chilling." Jewel lifted my chin and looked into my eyes. "If you're nervous, you can lie down here."

I wanted some time alone, and demurred, "That's sweet of you Jewel, but I think I'll go home. Dan told me to stay there. Maybe I should start listening to him."

"And to me."

"That, too."

When I got up to leave, Jewel gave me a hug and said, "Don't forget Brad's notes." She handed them to me. "Someday we'll look back on all this and laugh."

"I hope so. Maybe I'll see you later."

"That would be nice. I'll show you the new Tanzanite cabochons I got mail-order. Sleep tight, darlin'."

I looked both ways when I hit the sidewalk. No crazed murderers in sight. Inside my building and at my door, I heard Carlotta's voice.

"Meezfik!"

This, in Carlotta-speak, means Miss Vic. My super let her door slam shut; in a second it reopened, and Carlotta hustled toward me, carrying a huge arrangement of my favorite flowers: Casablanca lilies, tremendous six-inch porcelain-white blossoms. At current market price, twelve bucks a stem. I was impressed.

"What's this?" I asked.

"Zis coom fife, mebay it, meenoots. Seda infelop?" (These came five, maybe eight minutes ago. See the envelope?)

I opened the tiny white card. The flowers were from Sal, with a note reading, "Thanks for last night. Again?"

It was hard to believe we'd been at Windows on the World less than twenty-four hours before. It was harder to believe that Sal had the kind of class indicated by this floral gesture. But then, misjudging people seemed to be what I did best. I thanked Carlotta for signing for the bouquet, and took it into the apartment.

The lilies were too big for my living room, so they were relegated to a spot on the dining room table where I could still enjoy them. The heavy, sweet lily smell permeated the entire apartment. As I admired the arrangement, I dozed off.

Blub-blub-blub.

Blub-blub-blub.

The frog phone woke me. It was 7 P.M. I'd slept through the morning and the afternoon.

"Hello," I answered.

"Vic?" a man's voice asked.

"Yes." I paused. "May I help you?"

"Well . . . what a surprise!"

Who was this person?

"Vic, it's Sal."

"Oh, hi, Sal. Sorry, I was sleeping, and I'm still a little logy."

"Did you get the flowers?"

"Yes, Sal. They're my favorites; how'd you know?"

"I'm a real clever guy."

140

Brilliant. There was a pause. I couldn't think of a thing to say. Apparently, neither could Sal.

"I'm sorry I didn't call before to thank you, Sal, but—as I said—I fell asleep and the whole day kind of got away from me."

"That's cool."

Did I really hear a middle-aged man use the expression, "That's cool?" Again, I was at a loss for words. Sal bailed me out.

"Anyway, glad you like them. I didn't figure you'd be home; I was just calling to leave a message on your machine."

Now what could be the reason that Sal would assume I wouldn't be in my own apartment?

Sal continued, "A gorgeous woman like you, I figured you'd have a hot date."

Oh, yes, *that* reason.

"Well, Maximilian Schell had to cancel. Something about a last-minute Mozart concerto." Sal's puzzled pause led me to believe he'd never heard of Mozart, let alone Maximilian Schell.

"Anyway," Sal said, ignoring the entire esoteric reference, "I hope we can do it again real soon, Vic. Why don't I give you a call around the beginning of the week?"

My intercom buzzer erupted at that moment, saving me from having to say something knee-jerkingly fatuous like, "I'd love it."

"Someone's at my door, Sal. Let's talk next week."

"Terrif. You'd better check who's there while you've got me on the line. Better safe than sorry. I'll hold."

Terrif? A conversation with Sal was like being trapped in a 1960's surfer-movie script. He was right about safety, though, so I laid the frog on its side by the couch. Muscles protesting every inch of the way, I made it to my peephole to see who was at my door. Standing in the entrance light was a blond head. It was Lissa. Without thinking, I buzzed her in, and got myself back to the phone.

141

"It's Lissa, Sal. I've got to go. Bye." I hung up and went back to open the door.

"I've got to talk to someone, Vic, before I go crazy."

Lissa had one great entrance line there. I had the cloying feeling that I'd just done something abysmally stupid again, and was getting damned fed up with my feelings altogether.

"Come on in," I said.

"What do you know about David's murder?" Lissa asked.

"Nothing." The ugly truth was, I was so concerned about Barry, I'd just about forgotten entirely about anyone else.

"The hell you don't." Lissa forged past me into the living room. "Your husband is in jail for Kendall's murder, and under suspicion for David's. You and your boyfriend were first on the scene, when they found David's body."

"Second," I objected, "Frances was there first. Look, Liss, I know how it looks, but I don't know anything except that Barry never killed anyone. My apartment's been broken into by someone looking for God knows what, and some guy tried to beat my head in last night right in the hall. We're all upset here, but if you don't mind my saying so, *I'm* the next potential victim and, frankly, I hurt too much to have to go trying to prove it to you."

Lissa actually looked at me for the first time. The bruises on my neck and arms were livid against my fair skin. My hands were raw where they'd been cut on the glass shards.

The blonde collapsed into my wingback chair and covered her eyes with her hands. "I'm sorry, Vic. I'm just so upset. There's a lot you don't know." From beneath her fingers, she repeated, "I'm sorry."

"What don't I know?" I asked, going to her.

"Oh, it doesn't matter now."

"Maybe it matters a lot. I'm telling you, they've arrested the wrong person."

"Barry's a shit, Vic. I wasn't going to tell you, but he came on to me at the party, you know. Why are you trying to protect him? It's been on the news and in the papers. Barry

142

embezzled nearly four hundred thousand dollars from Kendall's accounts. Wake up, Vic. I wouldn't help him if he were hanging from the George Washington Bridge holding my wallet."

"What about me? Lissa, someone's stalking me. I don't think it's Barry, all he needs to do is call me and say, 'Yo, Red.' " I sighed at the truth of the statement. "Please. Maybe you know something that will help. What do you know that I don't?"

"Oh, lots," Lissa laughed. "The cops don't have an inkling either. You see, Kendall and I were having an affair."

Kendall and Lissa? Ogden and Frances? Kendall and Ogden? Dan was right, actors don't have enough to keep their hands busy.

"Lissa, I found out last night that David was having an affair with Frances. Did you know about that?"

"Oh, that's the best part."

"You told me Ogden was gay."

"I lied. David was as straight as you and me."

"But what about his fling with Kendall?"

"There wasn't one. That was a story that Ken and David let circulate to explain the amount of time they were spending together. You see, they were working on some projects for a couple of the networks. You know this business. There's not a story line in the world that's safe.

"It was David's idea for me to start sleeping with Kendall, while he schmoozed Frances." My astonishment read all over my face, because she explained further, "David and I were in love. The engagement started out as a publicity stunt of Dana's, but it ended up being true. Dana convinced us we had to wait if we wanted to get married, because it was obvious our fans didn't want it. That's when the shit started to hit the fan."

So Dana knew.

"What do you mean?" I asked.

"David became convinced that Kendall was just using him to get material for development with the networks. Ken started believing that he was destined to become a mogul. You know, creator, writing genius, and star: the Kevin Costner of the twenty-first century. David let it go, because Kendall had all the connections, but he thought we should both keep an eye on the Jameses. We did, from the horizontal position."

"I see," I nodded, not seeing at all.

"Then David started doing too many drugs. It was getting in his way on 'Raging Passions,' and Kendall wanted him gone so he wouldn't have to share any of the credit, should any of the projects come to fruition. Ken was leaving for California, and Dana wanted to fire David the minute he was gone.

"David complained to Kendall and threatened to expose him as a no-talent plagiarist. That's when Ken put the screws to Sal, and got David his audition for 'SPA!' As soon as David and I were established in California, we were going to get married."

"Lissa, did Kendall know about you and David?"

"I don't think so. He didn't even know for sure about David and his wife." Lissa leaned back into the chair. "But she, Frances, knew about us. It was awful. Just awful."

"Lissa, who do *you* think murdered Kendall and David?"

"I wanted to believe it was Barry. If it was, this nightmare would be over now. But I don't. I think it was Frances," she answered.

I was more confused than ever. Lissa's story made a good case for Frances's killing Kendall, but that couldn't explain David's murder. Or why I was attacked.

I stood up. "Frances was with Dan—Sergeant Duchinski—and me when David was killed. She couldn't have done it."

"Oh, Vic, grow up. Haven't you ever heard of murder for hire?" Lissa leaned toward me for emphasis. "Wouldn't that be perfect? Some thug does the deed, and Frances could arrange to have an alibi every time. And who could be a better alibi than the cop investigating the case?"

It was true that Frances had called me in a frenzy just prior to, or during, David Ogden's grisly demise. That would explain the missing checkbook, too—that is, if people contracting a murder ever pay by check. It didn't seem sensible, even to me. What would you write on the stub?

"Lissa, do you think Barry really stole all that money?" I asked the question I'd been avoiding.

Lissa shook her head and looked at me sadly. "Don't you?" she asked. The phone sounded, blub-blub-blub. Lissa stood up and hugged me. "I'm sorry, Vic, but I do. You'd better get the phone." Tears welled in her eyes and she slipped out the door.

"Yes?" I said into the phone.

Dan's voice shot back at me, "Good, you're home. Stay there."

"Is Barry out?"

"No, but stay there anyway. His lawyers are working hard to arrange it. How you feeling?"

"All right. I slept the day away."

"Figured you would. Sleep some more. I'll talk with you tomorrow."

"Dan?"

"What?" he answered.

I was shocked. "Aren't you going to say no?"

"I'm too tired. What?"

"Nothing. It doesn't matter. Good night."

So there it was. I wanted to know "precisely everything," and I was getting there. It just goes to show that the greatest curse is to be granted one's fondest wish. But I still wouldn't believe Barry was either a thief *or* a murderer.

I hefted the Manhattan White Pages, found the listing, picked up the frog and dialed. The answering machine that picked up gave another number where Elaine could be reached.

It was Barry's number.

The hell with Dan. First thing in the morning I was going outside, like a real person, and somehow get the truth from Barry's oh-so-mathematically adept chippie.

I owed that much to an innocent man, didn't I?

Or did I?

145

CHAPTER
THIRTEEN

Out of small deference to Dan's professional advice, I took a cab downtown instead of walking to Barry's apartment. I simply couldn't bring myself to talk to "Lainie" on the phone, so I forced myself out the door at eight-thirty that Sunday morning, figuring to catch her before she went out to do whatever it is that short accountants do on weekends.

New York City is as close to being deserted early Sundays as it ever is—with the possible exception of Memorial Day weekend. The Palestinian cabbie nevertheless chose to drive as though he were pretending the streets were bumper-to-bumper for his own amusement: darting from lane to lane, running red lights, pumping his horn at blasé pedestrians. No doubt I'd stumbled into the undercover cab of a Shiite militiaman.

Given everything that had happened during the past week, I was objectively amused at the irony of my heart thumping loudly in my chest over the prospect of seeing something as benign as another woman in Barry's apartment. Let's face it: comparatively, it shouldn't have been such a big thing for a bona-fide walking target like me.

But it was.

The cab-driver-from-hell overshot Barry's building by a block, just nudging the meter up another twenty-five cents. Uncharacteristically, I decided if that was the biggest pain I was going to have that day, I was in luck. Since the cabbie didn't have change for anything so absurdly large as a ten-dollar bill, I had to run into the Korean grocery on the corner and buy some cookies. I was shortchanged, but not enough to make a stink in my weakened condition.

The doorman recognized me and let me pass. I guessed I still had some clout. I guessed wrong. What a surprise!

"Vic!" Elaine exclaimed, opening the door. "The doorman said you were on your way up."

"Yes, well . . ." I stood awkwardly, waiting to be let in.

"Barry's not here, Vic. Didn't anyone tell you?"

"I heard. It was all over the news, and Lissa stopped by."

"Well, I don't know when he'll be getting back, Vic," Elaine said, still blocking my entrance.

I wanted to hit her. I admit it.

"I want to talk to you, Elaine." No reaction. I went on, "May I come in?"

"Oh, of course. How silly of me," she answered, opening the door. A Himalayan cat wandered over to check me out. "That's Muffin. I didn't want to leave her alone while I waited here for Barry."

Muffin. This woman whom Barry had given keys to owned a purebred cat named Muffin. Barry was involved with a short woman who paid *money* for a *cat*. I'd found Slasher, crawling with fleas, mewling in the back alley. I supposed that said it all. I was so jealous I thought I'd burst a blood vessel.

"Then Barry isn't annoyed with you about your pointing out the missing money in the James's books?"

"Of course not, Vic. He knows I was just doing my job. I *told* the police it couldn't be Barry's doing. He knows that."

Barry got "annoyed" with me for running out of milk for his morning coffee. He became livid with rage over my sleeping past 8 A.M. My blood vessels bulged with uncloaked envy.

147

"Are you all right, Vic?" Elaine asked. "Can I get you a cappuccino?"

God, no. Whatever did I think I was going to accomplish by questioning Elaine?

"I'm fine, thanks." I pulled myself together. "By any chance, Elaine, do you know where Kendall's checkbook is?"

"You know, the police asked me the same question. No, I don't know. I had a file of all the canceled checks, but the police took custody of those along with the books."

"Were there any especially large checks drawn? Did you notice?" I queried.

"No. Nothing out of the ordinary. I paid all the major bills—credit cards, mortgages, utilities—and made investments. The police have all the records, Vic. What are you getting at?"

"I don't know," I mumbled, and took a deep breath. "I *know* Barry. There has to be an explanation for the missing money."

Elaine shook her head. "Don't you think I scoured those books? I went over them until I thought I'd go blind. Of course Barry's no thief, I just couldn't find the answer. I had to tell the authorities. The numbers were all there. I hope you don't blame me for admitting what the independent auditors found to be true. I'm as upset as you are. Barry and I were talking about getting married as soon as his divorce became final . . ."

I felt as if someone had kicked the wind right out of me. And, given the abuse of the past days, I knew *exactly* how that felt. For those of you who think it's possible to cry yourself out: you're wrong. At least I had the pride to take my running nose out of there. I stood, grabbed my purse, and headed for the door.

"Vic, I'm sorry," Elaine apologized. "I thought you knew. But it was thoughtless of me."

I turned. "It's not your fault, Elaine, really." I smiled that foolish smile of the utterly mortified and hustled down the hall. Once in the stairwell, I blew my nose and sat on the marble steps for several minutes, chastising myself for my masochistic idiocy. In the lobby, I even had the presence of mind to be embarrassed by the sympathetic look from the doorman as he held the polished brass-and-glass door for my clumsy exit.

I fled directly into the faces of Brad and his news crew.

"Vic!" Brad said.

I snuffled discreetly and answered, "Hi, Brad. What's going on?"

"Just setting up. I was going to call you"—sure, sure—"but I wanted to let the dust settle before getting a statement. Since you're here, though, we might as well do it now."

"Are you crazy? Who do you think I am?"

"You're the wife of the alleged murderer, Vic. Give me a break here. You must have known the press would be after you eventually. Just give me a couple of minutes on camera."

"I can't, Brad, I'm union." This argument was having no impact, I could tell. "And isn't it unethical to pay for interviews? Let's talk later." Brad blocked my escape.

"Someone's going to get you, Vic. It might as well be someone who cares." He paused for effect. I made a mental note to turn that phrase into a sampler for my living room wall. "Elaine is making her statement in a half hour. That's why we're all here."

"She's *what?*"

Brad walked me back into the lobby and lowered his voice. "She's Barry's fiancée, as well as a witness. This is what I *do*. Look out there, Vic. There are trucks from channels two, four, five, seven, nine, and eleven out there. I'm sorry, but it's our *job*."

Sorry or not—and I thought not—everyone seemed to be assiduously doing his job these days: Dan, Elaine, Brad, everyone. It was pretty clear. My job description had somehow become that of the supportive cuckolded wife. Not only was it a rotten position, the pay was lousy.

"All right, Brad, but I'm not answering any questions. I'll

make a statement, and I'm outta here. Comprende? Get a minicam in here before the other sharks smell blood."

"There's not enough light in here," Brad argued.

"I don't look so good, anyway, now do I?"

Brad really noticed me for the first time that morning and asked, "Are those bruises?" He was peering at my cheek and inspecting my arms.

"Just get the cameraman, Brad."

I had the doorman secure the outer door just in case word spread of exactly who the bedraggled redhead standing in the lobby was. Brad stood next to me, holding the microphone, when the camera started to roll.

"This is Victoria Bowering, wife of attorney Barry Laskin, who is accused in the murder of television personality Kendall James, and implicated in the second murder of 'Raging Passions' star David Ogden. I understand you have a statement, Ms. Bowering." He moved slightly to the side to make room for the close-up shot that was sure to follow. Nothing like some up-front and intimate blubbering to boost the ratings.

I looked into the lens and said, "My husband is innocent of all charges lodged against him."

There was a pause of a few seconds—agonizing seconds on television. Brad nodded at me to continue.

I looked at him and said, "That's all."

"Cut!" he ordered. "That's all? That's *all?* From a professional, that's all? I've had more conversation from you in a movie theater."

"I probably didn't feel like I was going to barf then. Now, Brad, let me out of here. I'll give you an exclusive when this mess is resolved." I pushed toward the exit.

"By then no one will care," he said.

"Bingo!" I answered, and walked out and through the mob that was assembling. Without thinking of Dan's instructions, I walked to the bus stop and took the M-104 north to my apartment. I wasn't in the mood to stop for doughnuts.

* * *

My answering machine was blipping like crazy—which meant I'd received tons of calls during my brief absence. One was from my mother (New Hampshire had been informed, she was distraught even though she always knew Barry was a shit); two from Dan (who sincerely hoped I was sleeping late); one from Dana (explaining why she was setting up an interview for me on "Entertainment Daily"—great press: wife of accused murderer of "Raging Passions" star, herself on soap); six newspapers, AP, UPI; and all the major news programs in the New York area. Oh yes, and one from the ubiquitous Sal Steinbeck.

I fed Slasher again, unplugged the phone, and went back to bed.

Blahhhhhhht.
The door buzzer ripped me out of my fitful nap.
Blahht. Blahht. Blahhhhhhhhhhhhhhhhhhhhhhhhhhhhhhhht.

I opened the door to a raging, sputtering madman. Slasher poked his nose around the corner from the kitchen, and then dived for cover. The maniac's balled fists and hunched shoulders did not bode well.

"*What,*" Dan projected through his teeth, "the *hell* are you using for *brains?* I mean," he said, tapping my forehead, "what have you got up there? *Suet?*"

I opted for the innocent approach with, "L'Oréal, Light Reddish Topaz, just to cover the gray." I knew exactly what he was talking about before he said it, hours ahead of my projected schedule.

"*Television?*" he bellowed in confirmation. "I tune in to the news at noon, try to choke down a little lunch, and what do I *get?* I'll tell you what. I get your *face* on *television.* Did I or did I *not* order you to stay in the apartment? *Did* I or did I *not* convey to you what kind of *sling* your butt is *in?* Have I been speaking into a vacuum, or *what?*"

"Dan, you're scaring Slasher," I offered calmly, hoping to quiet him down.

"*Fuck* Slasher." Dan strode into the bedroom, pulled the cat from under the bed, and stomped back to me, cat tucked under his arm. Slasher looked irritated, but much less than Dan did. "Oh, shit," he groused, more resigned, "you scared me to death. I had visions of finding you in little tiny pieces all over the room." He chuckled Slasher under the chin. "The boy, too."

"Barry's out?"

"Yeah, yeah. His shysters were better than our shysters. He's out." Dan clutched Slasher so tightly the animal squeaked and wriggled away. "You got some coffee?"

"In the thermos. I'll get you some."

"Forget it. I'm too tense as it is." Dan leaned his head against the wall behind the sofa and closed his eyes.

"I had to see Elaine, Dan. I needed to hear her tell me that Barry didn't steal that money."

"Did she?"

"No." I shook my head, humbled.

"I didn't think she could. She was on the broadcast right before you, saying about the same thing. 'Barry is innocent.' Jesus, what does that guy have anyway? You're both intelligent, attractive women."

"I'm prettier," I asserted, praying he wouldn't argue about *that*.

"But you're both wrong." Dan crossed his arms. I sat next to him and rubbed his temples. We sat that way for several minutes, until Dan opened his eyes and looked at me. He reached over, wrapped his arm around my waist, tangled his right hand in the back of my hair, and kissed me like I haven't been kissed since high school.

It was an amazing experience, considering I'd known Dan for nearly a year.

After an exquisite, hormone-pumping interlude, he broke away and told me, "I don't care if you're married. Technically married, or really married, I don't care."

Gee, I wished he hadn't said that. That one "married"

152

word brought me abruptly back to real life. I'd actually come to hate real life. All I could say was, "Dan . . ."

"When Barry's in the slam for good, we're going to have to talk," he murmured. "I should go."

I sat up, not taking my eyes from Dan's face. Despite my best intentions, I'm certain I was wearing an I'll-never-under-stand-men-if-I-live-to-be-older-than-God's-mother look.

I said, "Do you mind if I have some coffee? All I seem to be doing lately is sleeping."

"Go ahead. I have to be getting back to the station anyway."

So much for romance.

"If you *have* to," Dan continued, "you can go out now. We've got three guys on Barry around the clock, with strict orders that he's not to get within ten blocks of your place."

"Thanks." I wasn't all that grateful.

"*But,*" he finished, "if you *have* to go out, don't go alone, and take the Mace. Okay? Okay."

I nodded at the closed door, and ran for the phone. There was no answer at Barry's. No doubt he'd disconnected his line, as I had, to avoid slime-o newspeople like Brad. After my stupid acquiescence to appear on TV, it would be just a matter of time before the cameras were perched on my front stoop, too. Carlotta would go nuts.

I went to get that cup of coffee I so desperately needed. It had to be the stress; I was yawning again. Slasher was pleased with my disorientation. I fed him for the third time that day.

Blahhhhhhhhhhhhhhhhhht.

CHAPTER
FOURTEEN

B*lahhhhhhhhhhhhhhht. Blahhhhhhhhhhhht. Blahht. Blahhht.*

If that was Brad, I was going to rip off his face and hand it to him. I never dreamed he would rush that tape at such breakneck speed to the studio for airing. Hell, I couldn't even figure out how it could have been edited. I took a long sip of black coffee, and set the cup aside. I didn't want anything breakable nearby, just in case.

Blahhhhht. I was hating the whole world at that moment. Maybe, most of all, my landlord and his sleazeball phony subcontractors—owned by him, of course—who installed grade triple-Z equipment at triple-A prices. *Blahhhhhhht.* I cracked the peephole and squinted down the long corridor to see who was there.

Blahhhhhhht. It was Sal, and I wasn't in the mood. *Blahhhhhht. Blahhht.* I thought it over. *Blahhhht.* I most definitely had no interest in fighting off Sal's amorous advances.

Blahhhhht. And I could use some more sleep. *Blahhht.* Yet, I was still convinced that I could figure out who really *did* murder Kendall. Sal might know something he didn't realize. *Blahhhhhhhhhhhhhhhhhhhhht.* And if that buzzer didn't stop soon, I was going to have to rip it from the wall with my bare hands. *Bla—* I buzzed Sal in.

"How'ya doin'?" Sal asked rhetorically. "Look!" he flourished a large Zabar's deli bag. Slasher was tantalized, ran up, and stuck his pink nose in the orange-and-white sack. "Your cat?"

Whose cat would it be? I reconsidered ripping the intercom about of the wall rather than spending time in a stupid conversation with a witless man.

"Nah," I answered. "Mine's in the shop. This one's a 'loaner.' "

He slowly digested the comment.

"Very good, Vic. That's very good. A 'loaner.' " Sal dropped the bag, narrowly missing Slasher's head, and sat on the arm of a chair. "How'ya feelin'?"

"I've been better." That was it! I could pretend to be sick! No man wants to neck with a woman who could puke at any moment.

"Yeah, those are ugly bruises ya got there. But you're safe now, aren't ya? Must be some relief." I acknowledged that it was, even though I knew better. "Look! I got a ton of junk at Zabar's—lox, bagels, cream cheese, goose liver, French bread, Brie, pickles, those little spinach-and-feta turnover things. I figured you must have some case of cabin fever by now, so whaddya say, how 'bout a picnic in Central Park?" I was at a loss for words, so Sal filled in for me, "Ya need a break here. It'll take your mind off your troubles. Or should that be Barry's troubles?" He chuckled heartily at his cleverness.

He was right about distracting me, though. It wasn't working yet, but who knows for sure about the future?

Stupid question.

"You're convinced the police have the right man, aren't you, Sal?" I asked.

"You're not? After everything they've found out? You are *some* woman, that's all I've got to say."

Terrific. I'd encouraged him. Of course, that's not to say there was any way to *dis*courage a man like Sal. "Barry said you hung on like a pit bull. Guess he was right about something, huh? C'mon, put on some shoes and shorts."

So what the hell, I did.

We walked east on Eightieth Street. My block had defiantly snubbed gentrification, but halfway down the next block, old brownstones shouldered one another proudly. Some painted brown, some white, an occasional green or royal blue—less garish that it sounds. The honey locust trees became progressively larger as we neared the better neighborhood of the park.

The afternoon had become oppressively hot and humid. The sidewalks radiated heat like a grill. On Columbus Avenue, with the Victorian Gothic Natural History Museum on our right, we turned left and uptown. The Haagen Dazs ice cream shop was featuring a special: ice cream cones for a mere $2.50. Only one scoop, but you had your choice of cake- or sugar cone.

When we hit Eighty-first, and took another right to head into the park, I made Sal stop so I could tie my hair up off my neck. Ringlets sprang as if by magic in a perverse halo around my face. Too cute for words, but I felt better even if I still looked like an over-the-hill Shirley Temple wanna-be. Sal was right about what I needed, after all.

Our most death-defying feat remained, however: to navigate through the kamikaze bicyclists, roller-bladers, and baby-buggy wielders into the Central Park entrance. I came within inches of being creamed by a bozo on a skateboard blowing a whistle. Sal pulled me aside in the nick of time, and we decided to walk along the grass on the shoulder.

"Caught you on the lunch news. You should try and get

over this obsession you have about Barry's innocence, Vic. It's unhealthy. It's time for you to get on with your life," Sal said, as we approached the softball fields.

"I can't, Sal. I'm loyal as a hound." I grinned at him to communicate my self-deprecating humor, but he wasn't buying any, so I asked the first thing that came into my head. "Did Kendall have any financial problems that you knew of?"

"Are you kidding? Kendall had fewer money problems than anyone I know."

"He had a percentage of your show, didn't he? That would have brought in a lot of cash almost right away, right?"

"Where did you hear *that?*" Sal asked.

"Well"—I thought about it—"I guess I didn't. Maybe I just assumed . . ."

"People shouldn't assume things. 'SPA!' is my baby. I might have cut Kendall in for a piece of the action after the first season, but we had absolutely no agreement to that effect. Don't you think being the star of a hit series is enough?"

Great. I'd pissed Sal off. These creative-genius types take a lot of energy to cosset.

"It'd be enough for me. But then, I'm nobody." I smiled again. Sal visibly relaxed.

"You're the only person who thinks Barry didn't do it," he reminded me sternly.

"I guess you're right," I admitted. Just enjoy the moment, play nice, I told myself. "Look, there's a game going on. Can we watch for a while?"

"Sure," Sal answered. He was probably happy to change the subject himself.

We sat down on the dusty grass off third base. The lawns were already yellowed and dry as hay. Sal looked profoundly uncomfortable, but humored me. Radios were blasting all around us, mostly in Spanish. Oddly enough, since I couldn't understand the words, the blare was easy to ignore. Babies fussed and squawled, miserable in the heat. Sal was sweating like a pig. I, of course, was merely glowing.

157

"Hey," I enthused, "I know that guy at bat."

"The fairy?" Sal asked. Even though actors talk like that all the time—especially the fairies—his tone offended me. But then, I was in "a mood."

"We did *Best Little Whorehouse in Texas* together for two months in Hazleton, Pennsylvania, of all places. Mark was my favorite Aggie dancer. *Go, Mark!*" I yelled. Sal scooched away from my cheer, and Mark struck out. I hoped my scream hadn't distracted him. The teams switched sides. "We can go now, if you want. It's pretty hot here in the sun."

"Thought you'd never ask," Sal said, obviously relieved to be moving. "We'll find someplace in the shade."

We wandered aimlessly for a while. The turrets of the Delacorte theater, built like an ancient castle, peeked out from over the tips of a stand of maple and oak. Some birds were singing, but the most pervasive animal sounds were human mixed with the soft coo of pigeons. The rhythmic whooshing of traffic beyond the dense island of trees reminded me of the white noise created by the Atlantic Ocean back home on the coast of New Hampshire. Never had it seemed so far away to me.

We were following a narrow footpath, up an incline, framed with boulders and weeds. The heavily leafed branches formed a comforting tent above our heads, and the sun was—at last—held at bay. I lit a cigarette and plodded along. The heat, the din, the green canopy created a sensation much like that of being wrapped in an unutterably soft comforter. No doubt about it, I was thinking "nap" again. Shuffling along, I took a languorous drag off my cigarette.

Halfway through the exhale, the residual smoke was punched from my lungs when I landed, face first, on the side of the weedy path. My head had missed a three-foot rock by centimeters. I pushed the cigarette I'd dropped away from my hair, loosed from the ribbon and splayed around my face. The last thing I needed was to go up in a whoomph of flames. I grunted slightly, raising myself on one elbow and rolling over onto my previously bruised derriere. Clumsy, clumsy, clumsy. I was too resigned to being a klutz even to be embarrassed.

Thwack! My skull cracked against the packed dirt, my spine crooked unnaturally over the uneven surface of the path's edge where I sprawled.

"What the he—" I managed before my voice was abruptly muffled. I opened my eyes into the twisted grimace of Sal Steinbeck, inches from my face. He was kneeling—thick thighs to either side—over my body, one meaty hand on my mouth, the other painfully securing both wrists over my head.

Rape? Wonderful, I thought. What a truly stellar way to end the worst week of my life. Sal lowered his mouth, his hand over mine vised.

Then I got *worried.*

"Tough luck, Vic," Sal whispered closely. I could barely hear him over the rampaging children, whirligig auto alarms wafting over from Central Park West, and a cacophony of dueling boom boxes. "This has gone way too far. Now Lissa's dead, too, and it's *all your fault.*" My eyes widened in panic. Sal went on, "You just wouldn't let go. 'Like a pit bull,' Barry said, and he was *right.* It wasn't bad enough that you had to be sticking your nose into my business, but you had to drag innocent people in, too. Well, now you see where that got you. You are *guilty.*"

Other people say that, under these nasty imminent-death circumstances, their lives flash before their eyes. Mine didn't. I was thinking how I should have paid attention to developing my upper-body strength. I cursed the fact that my Swiss Army knife was buried somewhere in my purse with a million keys dangling from it. I hated myself for being the kind of yutz who was so uncoordinated, I didn't dare carry Mace because, as sure as God made little green apples, I'd be hospitalized for a self-inflicted gassing. I blamed myself for never having had a baby, or learning to type. I loathed everything I'd done in my life that didn't prepare me for *this.* Sal's voice interrupted my self-abuse.

"Everybody wants a piece of the action, Vic. That's what

got you where you are, and that's what got Kendall where he is. He comes up with one decent idea for a show, and he *wants a cut.* I'm the one who developed it. *I'm* the one who interested the backers. *I'm* the one who hooked the network. *I am the creator.* What's Kendall James now, huh? He's a pile of rotting meat, that's what. You said it, Vic, you're the only person who believes Barry's innocent. Your cop friend knows you're undependable—always in places you shouldn't be. So, welcome to The Rambles, Vic. Welcome to the place where they find a body a week. I don't have to stick Barry with your murder, because you stuck yourself!"

That was the moment I bucked. Long legs are strong legs: it's geometry. Like an unskilled horseback rider taking a poorly timed jump, Sal tumbled over my head as I swung to the side and to my knees. I had one leg under me to jettison my body upright for escape when he hit me again.

I went down like a giant redwood. Sal threw himself on my back, grinding my cheek into the dirt. I could feel the pebbles grind against my teeth as I tried to lever myself up to flip Sal off. The man was a monster. His body weight was more than enough to immobilize me. I didn't know if he had a gun or—and why did this frighten me more?—a knife, so I concentrated on keeping Sal enough off-balance that he couldn't get to his pockets. I was doing relatively well, too, until he flattened himself over me, top to bottom. My mouth kissed gravel once more.

Sal was reaching for a sturdy tree limb just off to my left, and I was rapidly running out of reserve. With a quick heave, he had it in his hand. In one deft move, he chucked the deadwood under my chin and held it from either side. It was then that I felt the scrape, and then steady pressure upward, against my windpipe. He moved his knees up my back, until they pinned my shoulders to the earth. My vision started to go, along with my oxygen supply. Choking, I realized that his new position also afforded him a more efficient position from which to crush my esophagus like a bothersome cockroach.

160

Still, my life didn't flash. In fact, all I could think was, Well, if I'm going to die in such an ignominious manner, I'm sure as hell glad I never bothered to quit smoking.

My hands clawed the Central Park dirt, composed of discarded chewing gum, soft-drink straws, industrial soot, and cigarette butts. *My* cigarette butt, too. My cigarette, actually.

I worried that Sal would break my back before I was asphyxiated. I worried that it would be weeks before my body was found. And—top of the list—I worried that the chemical accelerants in my cigarette were insufficient to have kept it burning for the lifetime it seemed that Sal had been trying to kill me.

I shut my eyes. The only view I had was of the filth I was lying in anyway. My fingers worked furiously over my head, searching, searching. Lack of oxygen was causing numbness. Even if I found the cigarette, would I be able to manage to . . .

There.

Thank you, R. J. Reynolds. I had the lit end. I must have been burned, but felt no pain. I manipulated the cylinder of tobacco into the cup of my fist, burning end out. With what must have been my last hurrah, I curled my back, kicking Sal's ass with my heels. He raised his head just enough.

Precisely as he lowered his face again to get back to the deadly serious business of strangulation, I thrust my hand straight backward as hard as I could, which wasn't very far, considering the arm was free only from the elbow down. There was a nauseating momentary sizzle that led me to hope that my cancer stick had made direct contact with Sal's nasty little eyeball.

His unearthly scream convinced me of it.

Sal got to his feet more swiftly than I believed possible— by scrambling full-weight across my spine. I pedaled away on my rear end from the flailing man, heels digging into the thin dirt and pushing crablike to temporary safety. My attacker was clutching his face, moaning in a low guttural animal sound.

Clear fluid ran from between Sal's fingers and over his left cheek. *Bingo.* I was on my feet in a shot, running as fast as my thirty-five-inch inseam would take me—which is pretty damned fast. I hadn't a clue where I was inside the park, so I followed the noise of humanity. I didn't care if it was a traffic jam or a picnic, I ran toward the din. Not more than a thousand yards over the hill was the theater-league softball game, still in progress.

I headed for the great American pastime like a tornado to a trailer park.

Time to scream, I told myself. Definitely time to scream. I could hear Sal's shouts and stumbling too close behind me to turn and double-check, so I just ran, thinking Scream, scream, scream, you asshole.

Fabulous. This self-loathing thing of mine was *way* out of hand. I remained mute, the only sound was of my labored wheezing.

My "Best Little" buddy, Mark, spotted me streaking toward the field. Scream, for God's sake, I reminded myself, and waved my arms just like a woman running for her life.

Mark smiled widely and waved back.

"Hey, Vic!" he yelled. "C'mon over!"

Why wasn't I screaming?

Mark commenced an athletic lope in my direction, pleased to see an old scum-buddy. That's when I fell like a bag of laundry at the end of a chute. My mouth moved, my vocal cords didn't. No wonder I wasn't screaming.

I couldn't.

Several of Mark's friends joined him in the circle around my prone body.

"Vic? What happened, Vic? Where you attacked?"

I nodded.

"Somebody call nine-one-one!" Much noise and confusion. "Vic? Who did it? Is he still out there?"

I nodded.

162

"I put a cigarette in his eye," I croaked, after what seemed an eternity of struggle. "Can't miss him."

I watched half a dozen pairs of well-muscled dancers' legs dash off in the direction of Steinbeck. Mark called over the pitcher from the opposing team, *Cats,* I think, relinquishing custody of my battered form to the Mr. Universe ministrations of I-didn't-catch-the-name.

Then, I hope for the last time, I kissed the ground.

CHAPTER
FIFTEEN

I am not staying here!" I shouted as best as I could manage through my bruised larynx. I sounded like Bea Arthur.

"Yes, you *are!*" Dan easily shouted back louder. "The doctors insist on holding you for observation. You may have a concussion."

"Well," I rasped aggressively, sort of going with the Bea Arthur thing, "when I inform hospital administration that I have no medical insurance, I'm sure they'll see it my way."

"You don't have insurance?" Dan was appalled.

"I'm an actor," I said, explaining it all in that one phrase. "Now tell me, how did you catch Steinbeck?"

"We didn't. By the time we got to the scene, the ambulance was there and Sal was being held hostage by the male chorus of *La Cage aux Folles,* screaming for AIDS testing."

"You're kidding." I grinned.

"Nope. You punctured his eye, by the way."

My stomach lurched. "I know." Before I could get another lecture, I added, "I should have brought the Mace."

"Thank you," Dan said, vindicated. "We had Steinbeck's hotel suite searched and came up with the missing checkbook, but there are a couple of things we still don't understand. Sal refuses to say why. See, without being able to prove a strong motive, Steinbeck is going to have the option of copping an insanity plea. He could be out in about as much time as it takes to put him in. We're not having any luck there, I'm afraid. The son of a bitch is doing everything in his power to establish that he is, and always has been, crazy as a shit-house rat.

"The good news is at least we know how he pulled it all off. Seems our buddy worked his way through school doing all kinds of odd part-time jobs. One of them was with a locksmith. It was no problem for him to pick the lock on the Jameses' co-op, or—and don't gloat about this—spike the exterior lock mechanism with an especially virulent poison."

"And he worked for a a pharmacist, too, I remember him telling me over dinner," I interjected hoarsely.

"Right," Dan agreed. "He knew that to secure the interior dead bolt, Kendall always hung the keys from his teeth to locate the proper one. That's why all James's pocket stuff was lying around him just inside the door." I waited patiently until he finished with, "So you were right, okay? I'll go tell the doctor it's okay to release you. You don't seem all that befuddled to me." He patted my arm. "At least no more than usual."

Dan walked out into the corridor, leaving me alone with my thoughts. Despite Dan's pronouncement of my intact mental faculties, I was having a hard time pulling the past several hours into focus. Besides that, I really needed a cigarette. I reached under the hospital bed, pulled out my purse, which the nurse had put there, and stuck an unlit butt between my lips. It seemed to help. Some.

Pieces of Sal's ramblings during the attack filtered through the fog, like daylight. Lissa. Something about Lissa . . . Dan came back into the institutional-green room and dropped his weight in the chair next to my bed.

"The release papers are coming," he said.

165

"Good." I looked around the bare hospital room to see what I needed to gather. Even though I'd only been a recuperating resident for a matter of hours, there wasn't much to take. It was probably my long history of cleaning out dressing rooms that made me think of it. "You know, if Sal weren't in the slammer, I'd have some flowers to bring with me. *He* sent flowers even though he wanted me dead." Mindlessly, I ran down the list of people who should have sent floral tributes. Certainly the show-biz folk. Until my role call hit a name like a truck into a snow bank.

"Dan?"

"Yes." Not the question "Yes?" but the answer "Yes."

That stopped me in my tracks. A yes, from Dan? My heart sank, but I plunged ahead anyway, "You don't know the question."

"I do, though. And I'm sorry, Vic. Steinbeck killed Lissa last night in her apartment." He reached over and took my hand. "He heard that Lissa showed up at your place yesterday night, when you had him on the phone." A phlegmy wad of guilt obstructed my throat. "He knew about her and Ogden, and Ogden's working with Kendall," Dan went on to explain. "It looked to him like you were on the verge of putting together his involvement with all of them. If you didn't, he knew Lissa was bound to, eventually."

"Oh, God," I moaned. Dan would not release my hand so that I could cover my eyes.

"It wasn't your fault, Vic. Nobody suspected Steinbeck. He seemed to be the one with the most to lose over the murders."

"But why kill Ogden? If he hadn't murdered him, too, Lissa and I wouldn't have gotten so much more involved."

"We don't really know why. The randomness of the victims works in his favor to establish him as a nutburger." He kissed my hand and stood, stretching his arms and slowly pacing the tiny cubicle.

"So who was the man who attacked me in my hall?" I asked.

166

"Paid help. Steinbeck really liked you, Vic. He was hoping you'd back off. The night you had dinner, it became clear to him that you weren't going to. Before he sent you home with his driver, he called some friends. You'd be amazed at how many 'friends' of that sort are in your industry. Again, Sal had no trouble providing access to your building, since he had already thoughtfully provided his henchman with a dupe of your key. Zip, zip, and the bad guy was in. If you'd gone to Sal's hotel room like a good girl, he'd have called the hit off. Or at least postponed it. But another thing we *don't* have yet is why your apartment was tossed, unless it was just to scare you."

Wham. The pieces fell into place. "No, it wasn't to frighten me. At least not entirely. Sal was looking for the notes I'd gotten from Brad Sinclair. I took them over to discuss with Jewel, and forgot them there—but he didn't know *that.* When they didn't turn up during his search, he figured he'd take me to dinner and pump me!"

"So to speak," Dan intoned dourly.

The doctor walked in with a pile of papers and said, "No smoking inside this hospital Ms.—uh—Bowering."

I snapped the cigarette from my mouth. Regaining my composure, I said, "I'm not smoking. I am fulfilling a juvenile oral need. See?" I held up the unlit cigarette. "Dead as a doornail."

Unimpressed with my state-of-the-art good behavior, she continued, "I don't advise this discharge. You should stay here at least twenty-four hours, so we can monitor you for any signs of concussion. Nothing showed up on the X rays, but you never know."

No, you never do.

I reached for the papers. "I don't have any medical insurance," I said, looking over the pile.

"But if you insist," the doctor finished her spiel in the finest tradition of Neil Simon, without taking a beat, "sign here"—she pointed—"and here, and here. Initial here, here, and here."

I did, posthaste.

"A nurse will be here in a few minutes with a wheelchair. Hospital regulations. Try to stay off your feet. If you experience any double vision or nausea, please report it to your personal physician. Good luck."

"What a warm and wonderful woman," I croaked after she'd left the room. Miraculously, a nurse swept through the door with my transportation immediately. Dan helped me into the chair, a little surprised I wasn't arguing about it, I believe.

"I'll have a patrol car take us back to your place. I'll get you settled, and then I have to get to an appointment," Dan said, shrugging off the nurse and propelling me himself.

Maybe my injuries had jogged something loose. Wouldn't it be a horrible joke if my psychic tendencies had improved with near death? I knew he was going to Barry's.

"Dan?"

"No. Absolutely not. You are going home and to bed. There is nothing you can do now." He pushed faster, jaw set.

I didn't notice the lapse in verbal communication at that time, but continued, "Yes, there is. It's in those canceled checks and Barry's records. You got the copies from the bank, didn't you?"

"No," he lied, flagging down a police car and flashing his detective's shield.

"If you don't take me, I'll take the bus," I threatened. "I'll *walk*. Hell, I'll *jog,* Dan, you know I will." My throat felt as if I'd swallowed lye.

"Don't I ever," he conceded as the flagged car pulled up beside us. "All right, but I think you're just going to end up more upset than you are already."

"I'm not upset." And I wasn't. The final answers were to be found hiding in the papers at Barry's apartment. I knew it. "Dan? Could we take the bus? I want to look at people. You know?"

Dan sighed, "I know," and told the police they could go on their way.

The sun had gone down and taken the temperature with

it. It was too hot to sleep, but blissfully comfortable for sitting and just breathing. I was moving at a pace a three-toed sloth could beat, but the bus stop was just across the street from St. John's. It was for the right route assignment, too, my old friend the M-104 downtown.

I unzipped my purse to pull out tokens. The least I could do was treat.

"Never mind," Dan stopped me. "Some good Samaritan stole your wallet while you were out of it."

A bus pulled up at that moment. One look at me, and the driver automatically lowered the entrance side to curb level. Even at that, Dan had to support me up the four short stairs. He pulled out his own tokens and dropped them into the change slot, while I staggered unsteadily toward the back of the crowded transport. I found my spot and lowered myself carefully.

"Steinbeck keeps saying it was all your fault," Dan said, hanging from the balance bar above my head, "and I'm inclined to believe him."

"Yeah, well, he *still* sent flowers. There's a lot to be said for that," I teased.

"Alibi. Covering his ass and contributing circumstantial evidence that he didn't know you'd been whacked."

I repositioned myself in the hard plastic scoop that served as bus seating, enjoying the blast of arctic air-conditioning coming from the fan next to the rear exit door. This particular seat on the new NYC transit buses is my favorite for two reasons. One, the position of the fan makes the spot colder than a pederast's soul; and two, because of this flash-freeze aspect, the seat is almost always empty.

"So you believe me now, after all?"

"That Barry didn't kill James, Ogden, or Lissa? Yes," Dan responded, taking the seat that became available to my left. He bumped my arm.

"Ouch."

"Sorry. But the embezzlement charges stand, Vic. Maybe

we'll find something in those canceled checks to put another nail in Sal's coffin, but I think your hubby's cooked."

I leaned back into the refrigerated air, took Dan's hand, and watched upper Broadway waltz by. Every two blocks, the bus stopped for passengers. For forty minutes, I enjoyed the people. First, Harlem with its black faces, crowded stoops, noise, and children cavorting in open fire hydrants. Then Columbia University with its diverse mixture of young and old of every ethnic group, bookstores, coffee shops and fast food. At 108th Street, the panorama settled into familiarity—the good old Upper West Side, trendy restaurants becoming more frequent as we traveled south, along with fashionable boutiques. Grocery stores started to disappear, replaced by more boutiques and a staggering variety of women's shoe stores and copy centers. The prices displayed at the Korean greengrocers' climbed higher and higher.

As the bus rolled past the most popular vegetable market in the city, I noted with affection the old ladies shoving their way in front of businessmen, who elbowed them back—usually without success. Baby strollers clogged the open aisles and blocked access to the displays of fruit set up on the sidewalk. Plastic produce bags fluttered from their rolls in the breeze and blew into the gutters and down the street, catching on the shoes of pedestrians, who shook them off irritably. A bum at the one exit door shoved a cardboard cup in the nose of everyone who managed to get out of the interior. I was vividly reminded of every New Yorker's friend, the roach motel. "Shoppers check in . . . but they can't get out!"

I looked over and caught Dan watching me with concern.

"I'm all right, Dan, really."

"No, you're not. There's nothing you can do for Barry; it's time to get on with your life."

"I am," I protested.

"You still love him," he stated, and stared across the aisle and out the window. "He's engaged to someone else, and he's probably going to be in the slammer for some time."

"No, he isn't."

"Vic . . ." Dan paused for a moment and began again, patiently, "Okay, even if he doesn't serve time, you can't expect anything from him. You know that, don't you?"

I turned to look at the enormous golden statue at Columbus Circle. "I know that." And I thought I believed it.

But I didn't.

We sat in silence until Dan pressed the strip of luminescent tape that triggered the bell and sign at the front of the bus to tell the driver we wanted to get off.

"Can you make it?" Dan asked when the bus stopped.

"And what is my alternative, Sergeant?" I smiled. Dan preceded me and held the door open. Every step down felt like a bungee-cord jump from the top of the Empire State Building, but I made it.

At the entrance to Barry's building, we were met by a Lieutenant Arnold.

"Took you long enough, Sergeant," Arnold said, tucking a portfolio case under his arm and heading to the door.

"It was a hostage situation, Lieutenant," Dan quipped.

"Funny, Duchinski. Let's get on with this."

Dan flashed his shield at the doorman and told me, "This is Lieutenant Arnold, Vic. He's our ace number-cruncher, on loan from the Feds." To Arnold he said, "Did you get the bank copies of Laskin's transactions?"

"If I hadn't, would we be here?" came the reply.

What a sweetheart. I have to say that I hadn't been meeting a lot of social animals lately.

Barry answered the door himself.

"Vic!" he said the moment he saw me, "thank God. They wouldn't let me come to the hospital." Barry shot Dan a dangerous look, which was not very clever, given the circumstances. Dan ignored him with the kind of self-composed tolerance specific to cops and bartenders, and went with Arnold to the living room. "Are you all right?" Barry asked.

"Compared to what?" I joked in what I hoped was a hail-fellow-well-met way. I looked around. "Where's Elaine?"

Barry paused, for the first time in his life seemingly at a

171

loss for words. "She's left me. She waited until I was released, though," he defended her bravely. "She couldn't take it anymore. I can't say that I blame her."

Barry looked so destroyed, I couldn't even take pleasure in his misery.

"Can we get to this, please?" shouted Arnold.

"I'm sorry, Barry," I said, and we joined the men in the living room. I saw that Elaine had rearranged the furniture into a "conversation pit" configuration—rather an East Side sensibility, if you ask me.

"Arnold," Dan led, "if it's all right with you, I'd like to start with the Jameses' checkbook. Ms. Bowering here thinks there's something to be found in it, and—as you can see—she belongs in bed. The sooner we can get that out of the way, the sooner she can get home."

"Doesn't matter to me," Arnold shrugged, pulling the faux-leather checkbook from within the portfolio. I sat down, and he shoved the checkbook across the brand-new glass-topped oversized coffee table.

That peculiar buzz spread up from my fingertips as I lifted it from the surface of the table. This was it. This was *definitely* it.

"She's getting something," I heard Barry tell Dan. "She had the same look the night she was cheating at Trivial Pursuit."

"She looks blind," commented good-old-boy Arnold.

"Are you okay, Vic?" Dan asked me.

"Fine, fine," I answered, opening the book to the white record-keeping portion, and running my fingers down the columns. I didn't close my eyes, but Arnold was right. I wasn't seeing anything.

"Jesus," Arnold said with disgust, and started rifling through the papers in his portfolio case.

"Shhhh," Barry whispered. Dan remained silent.

I blinked twice, and looked down to see what had stopped my finger. It was a check made out seven months before for twenty dollars. *Twenty* dollars?

172

The check was made out to be payable to the Library of Congress. *Yes!*

"This is it." I grinned. "This is the motive for Kendall's murder. And I'll just bet it's a damned good case for the killing to be about as premeditated as they come."

"The Library of Congress?" Dan asked.

"Of course," Barry broke in. "That's the fee for copyrighting of material. Kendall had a script copyrighted. Where are those canceled checks?" Arnold handed over an brown-paper accordion case. Barry leafed through until he found the check in question. "I knew it."

Dan took the check from Barry and examined it. Written on the line marked "for": was the notation "SPA!"

"Kendall was fastidious about everything," Barry said.

"Except what he put in his mouth," amended Dan dryly. "Well, it'll be easy enough to get a copy of the material from the Library of Congress. You can get on that, can't you, Arnold?"

Arnold nodded slowly, and looked at me as if I'd just grown horns and a tail. Dan merely crooked an eyebrow. I crooked mine back.

"May I?" I asked, picking up Barry's records without waiting for permission. My head jerked up.

"You knew!" I accused the lovable Lieutenant Arnold.

"What?" Barry trilled. "What?

"Let me see those," Dan demanded, taking them from my hands. He flipped through the pages rapidly, comparing figures from time to time with the account books provided by Elaine.

"How did you do that?" Arnold asked me.

"Damn!" Dan swore emphatically. "You *did* know, Arnold. The money didn't disappear from Laskin's end. It got siphoned off at the accountant's. Why didn't you inform me?"

"I just got the bank copies last night, Duchinski. I think what remains to be proved is whether or not Laskin was in cahoots with his fiancée. We're talking about almost half a million here."

173

"That's why she left me," Barry muttered to himself.

"What? Speak up, Laskin," bullied Arnold.

"Elaine left him as soon as he got out on bail," I said softly. Waves of hurt and humiliation washed from Barry to me. I didn't go to him. It would have been more than either one of us could have borne.

Arnold looked doubtful. "Why'd she hang around *that* long?"

"Probably thought it wouldn't look good to disappear immediately," muttered Dan.

Barry shook his head in weary disagreement. "Jewish guilt." He looked out the window, envisioning God knows what. "She's really a very moral person."

"Well, we'll just see about that, won't we?" Arnold said. "I don't suppose you have any idea where your fiancée—ex-fiancée," he corrected himself, "might be just now."

"She said she was going to Montauk to think," Barry mumbled.

The last time Elaine went to Montauk to "think," she'd come back with a dummied set of books.

"Why am I so sure she's not in the country?" Dan questioned no one in particular.

"Well," Arnold the Fed grunted as he stood and placed everything back in his portfolio, "looks like you lucked out, Laskin. My experts tell me the books were faked all at once. That means your cuddle-bunny probably made the decision to abscond *after* Kendall was murdered. You were pretty busy around that time, weren't you?

"We'll see. I don't think we'll have any trouble picking her up. She's not exactly a career criminal, so we'll get the story out of her." Arnold marched to the door. "I'll let myself out. Laskin, just don't be taking any trips to Zimbabwe without letting me know, okay?"

Barry nodded dully. Arnold left.

"Are you all right, Barry?" I asked.

He nodded again, and stared out the window at the lights of the city.

174

"Is there anything I can get you?" I tried.

He shook his head slowly, his eyes riveted on those lights.

"I'm going home now, Barry," I said, standing, using Dan's shoulder as a prop. "Call if there's anything I can do."

Barry just stared without blinking, as Dan helped me out the door.

EPILOGUE

Dan assigned Carlotta the task of taking care of me for the week following Sal's arrest. So assiduously did she take on her responsibility, I took to calling her "the Bitch of Buchenwald." I only had the courage because I said it very quickly and slurred my professionally precise pronunciation. On the rare occasions Carlotta allowed Brad into my apartment with flowers, he found it screamingly funny. But when he laughed too enthusiastically, she took to cracking him on the top of his head with whatever junk novel I was reading at the time. Being a smart man, he learned to stifle his mirth. And, of course, given the newest fiscal crisis in the New York City government, he didn't come by very often.

Dan dropped by every day, ostensibly to cheer up Slasher, but managing to make me feel better, too, no matter what he said. I asked him how he always knew what it was I needed on a given day—one time a Snickers bar, another time pistachio nuts, once a squirt gun.

"Mind readers have two choices," Dan explained, "the

bar-mitzvah circuit . . . or law enforcement. Think about it."

I didn't have to. I knew he was right.

Through it all, Carlotta stood guard, pronouncing with every male visitor, "Bists. Zeral cheets." (Beasts. They're all shits.)

My under-five job on "Raging Passions" was given to the monolithic male with the red beard and the tattoo, since I was "indisposed." Olive called to say she might have something for me again early the next year, and that she'd call. I decided not to hold my breath.

It wasn't until two weeks after Mexican police had apprehended Elaine in Puerto Vallarta—how unimaginative!—that Barry took me to lunch. We went to a tiny outdoor café on Amsterdam Avenue and Eighty-first Street. The white resin (read "plastic") tables balanced precariously on the uneven sidewalk. The surface area of each was barely large enough for the place settings and a tiny vase of carnations. We both ordered Pernod and water, vichyssoise, soft-shell crabs, and decaf coffees. After ten years of marriage, not much of a surprise. Married couples are supposed to start looking the same; Barry and I simply started eating the same.

Barry walked me home. The heat had temporarily broken, the murder rate was back down, and my bruises had mostly faded to an unpleasant memory. When we reached the stoop he stopped, took my hands in his, and sat me down on the bottom poorly tiled terra-cotta step.

"I made a mistake, Vic."

"Was that *you?*" I joked.

"Not now, Vic, please," Barry said, looking at me so sadly I was afraid my heart would break right there, a foot and a half from the bright-blue recycling bin.

"Everyone misjudges people, Barry. It wasn't your fault. You were in a . . . bad time."

"That's right. It was an awful time. But it wasn't just Elaine, Vic. I'm . . ." He took a deep breath, "What I'm trying to say is that I misjudged *you.*"

"That's okay, Barry."

177

"No," he said quickly, then slowed down. "No, it isn't. Because when I misjudged you, I misjudged us. I love you, Vic."

"I love you, too, Barry."

"Will you forgive me?"

The pain radiated from his skin the way heat rises from a sun-baked beach. I could only tell him the truth.

"I forgave both of us a long time ago. Besides, it takes two to make a divorce." My sentiment embarrassed me. "And you are a shit, Barry. I'm a dilettante n'er-do-well, and you're a shit." My attempt at levity was misplaced.

Barry held my hand to his lips and spoke into my palm. "Will you come home? I need you at home, Vic."

I looked across the street. Billy, the jolly parking-garage attendant, waved to me. I smiled and nodded back. A garishly painted Camaro with blaring monster stereo cruised by, the strains of "La Bamba" drowning out the cooing of pigeons along with the drumming in my ears. I recited "Jabberwocky" to myself until I could answer like a grown-up.

"I *am* home, Barry."

He examined my eyes. "Yeah," he breathed. "Yeah." Barry stood quickly, kissed my forehead, and took several determined strides west, toward Broadway. He stopped in the shade of a young ginkgo tree, paused a moment, and turned.

Pointing at me, and waggling his finger, Barry shouted, "But I demand my visitation rights under the terms of our post-nuptual agreement!"

"What post-nuptual agreement?" I yelled back.

"The one I'm going back to my office to draft." He stood very straight, giving his most authoritarian bluster. "And I'll expect to have it signed by the end of this week, missy!"

Barry was already around the corner and marching up Broadway before I could move without a tremble and manage the tiniest nod of acquiescence.